Better

than Blonde

Teresa Toten

PUFFIN
CANADA

PUFFIN CANADA

Published by the Penguin Group

Penguin Group (Canada), 90 Eglinton Avenue East, Suite 700, Toronto, Ontario, Canada M4P 2Y3
    (a division of Pearson Canada Inc.)

Penguin Group (USA) Inc., 375 Hudson Street, New York, New York 10014, U.S.A.
Penguin Books Ltd, 80 Strand, London WC2R 0RL, England
Penguin Ireland, 25 St Stephen's Green, Dublin 2, Ireland (a division of Penguin Books Ltd)
Penguin Group (Australia), 250 Camberwell Road, Camberwell, Victoria 3124, Australia
    (a division of Pearson Australia Group Pty Ltd)
Penguin Books India Pvt Ltd, 11 Community Centre, Panchsheel Park, New Delhi – 110 017,
    India
Penguin Group (NZ), cnr Airborne and Rosedale Roads, Albany, Auckland 1310, New Zealand
    (a division of Pearson New Zealand Ltd)
Penguin Books (South Africa) (Pty) Ltd, 24 Sturdee Avenue, Rosebank, Johannesburg 2196,
    South Africa

Penguin Books Ltd, Registered Offices: 80 Strand, London WC2R 0RL, England

First published 2007

(WEB)   10 9 8 7 6 5 4 3 2 1

Manufactured in Canada.

ISBN-13: 978-0-14-305314-9
ISBN-10: 0-14-305314-0

Visit the Penguin Group (Canada) website at **www.penguin.ca**

Special and corporate bulk purchase rates available; please see **www.penguin.ca/corporatesales**
or call 1-800-810-3104, ext. 477 or 474

To Nikki,
my Sunshine

"Secrets are things we give to others to keep for us."

—*ELBERT HUBBARD*

Better

than Blonde

Prologue

I inhaled so sharply, it felt like I'd cut myself.

He was still beautiful.

I know that's a weird thing to say about a man—especially about your father—but he was, so there you go. For all those years, he was so handsome in my head. Whenever he started to dissolve around the edges, I'd spend hours poring over the photographs, staring at straw-coloured hair falling into laughing eyes. He was always smiling, he was always so . . . but I wasn't a child any more. I *knew* he'd look different. What if I didn't recognize him? Prison changes a man. I know that. I've seen all the movies. You can hardly tell it's Burt Lancaster two-thirds of the way through *Birdman of Alcatraz.*

He stood frozen at the far end of the penitentiary corridor.

I recognized him.

And he was still beautiful.

Mama nudged me along with her toward him. It seemed that Papa wouldn't or couldn't come toward us. We waded through the heavy air, which was thick with sweat and Lysol. Papa became crisper and clearer with every step. His blond hair was darkened here and there where he'd tried to tame it with too much Brylcreem. I instantly remembered that he had always done that. Mama made him. A small tobacco-coloured suitcase was on the floor to his right. A guard, clutching a sheaf of papers and smiling, stood well behind Papa to his left. Papa wore his navy blue suit, the nice one, the one we bought for the trial seven years ago. It was all too big. The crisp, white shirt had gaps where his neck should have been and the suit sleeves grazed his knuckles. Still, it was the suit that looked ill at ease, not Papa.

He didn't even blink. He was staring at me that hard. Mama was invisible to him.

As it should be.

He'd seen her the whole time, month after month. He hadn't seen me for almost three years. Papa drank in my steps, not hers, inhaled and exhaled with me, not her.

Jesus. *Stay light on your feet, Princess. Kill or be killed. Feint right, go left.* All that stuff that he was so wrong about. I was crackling with memories that splintered all around me. All the schools, all the stories, the fear of being found out, and then being found out. If only he hadn't been drinking that night—twenty more steps—but then again, I had abandoned him, lied about him. Those ugly, awful family visits to the penitentiary with its hideous men and us, the hideous families—ten more steps. But then, I had refused to come. And finally, all those wasted years for something he didn't even do but was too drunk to know that he didn't even do.

I couldn't sort out the shame. I kept ricocheting from *his fault* to *my fault* and back again.

The guard cleared his throat and a phone rang. It was like hearing it all under water. I stopped—no more steps. Papa clenched and threw open his arms, reaching for me.

And then I forgot. I forgot to be angry, to feel afraid, to be ashamed, and I charged into Papa, colliding deep into the navy suit. He crushed me, hugging so hard it hurt. I hugged back and he hugged tighter. Was there less of him, or just more of me? So much had changed, but everything was the same in Papa's arms.

"My baby, my Sophia," he was crying in my hair. "Princess, you've become a woman."

I couldn't breathe. It didn't matter. I'd breathe later.

Papa was coming home.

All the Blondes have diaries, gorgeous, perfect things that match their gorgeous, perfect selves. Madison's is bound in smooth, buttery-soft, turquoise leather. Her name is, ever so discreetly, embossed into the actual leather cover with silver that never tarnishes, and all the paper edges are dipped in the same supershiny silver.

Kit's diary is hard-core psychedelic. The cover is this thick, double-plastic sheeting, and trapped between the plastic sheets are these liquids that pool in and around each other and then separate. The puddles are all neon: neon orange, neon yellow, neon pink, neon green, and so on. It's not so much a diary as it is an entertainment centre.

Sarah's diary is covered in hot-pink, fluffy, rabbit fur. She strokes and plays with that thing the way Auntie Radmila plays with her rosary beads.

There must be this secret AMAZINGLY PERFECT DIARY STORE out there somewhere and you have to be a Blonde to have the address.

It's okay. I hate to write.

Especially about me.

The Blondes go on and on about all the bits of their lives, all the highlights, all the lowlights. I don't even want to *think* about my bits, let alone write them down on paper—the lies, the moves, the schools, Mama's catatonic episodes—*who* would write that down?

Kit says that it's perfectly acceptable to just draw up lists of things and date them, and then it'll end up being, like, this perfectly preserved record of who and what you were at that moment in time.

Well, that just gives me the sweats.

You jot a few things down in a moment of weakness, and there they are, trapped on a page to mock you and your seriously shallow self forever. Sarah says any kind of list will do: favourite songs, guys you like, self-improvement goals. They all freak me out. Well, except for the guy thing. There is the ever-luscious, heart-poundingly gorgeous Luke Pearson. But then again, the love of my life is apparently still dating Alison double-D Hoover, and who needs to see that down in black and white?

The song lists don't work either.

I know from past experience that I start out all honest and real, and then it hits me that if this gets out, I'm beyond ruined. It'd be easier to survive school with everyone knowing that Papa was in the Kingston Pen than with everyone knowing that Abba's "Dancing Queen" made it to my number-two spot.

The self-improvement thing is worse. I mean, where do I begin? No, it's not even that. The thing is, I'm just smart enough to be ashamed of my goals. See, what I really, really deep down, kind of want, badly . . . is to be a Blonde. There are times I could burst a kidney for the sheer wanting of it.

Oh, not the hair thing. I know nothing's going to transform my wiry black mop into straight sheets of sunlight, though, Jesus God, wouldn't that be great! No, what I want is to be a Blonde in the deeper, metaphysical, spiritual sense, with a big honking house, fabulous clothes, and a shimmery blonde life with no complications. Okay, so I now know that even Blondes can be a bit complicated, but they also have soft-spoken families who discuss their day over roast beef and parsnips at real dining room tables with a father who's always smiling indulgently at them.

Well, as of a few weeks ago, I now have a father who smiles at me indulgently non-stop. So . . . it would be ungrateful or greedy, or something like that, to admit to still wanting to be a Blonde.

So . . . I won't.

Besides, I don't have a diary. *Didn't* have a diary.

I must have made the mistake of telling Papa about those incredible diaries at some point over the summer.

I'll have to watch that.

Papa was in prison for almost seven years and clearly feels compelled to fulfill every possible desire I might have had, have now, or am thinking about maybe having.

So, I now have a diary.

I am the proud owner of a one-of-a-kind work-of-art diary that was entirely designed and constructed by my father. Papa is profoundly creative. I forgot about that part.

He hand-cured and tanned the leather himself, and then he went and made the paper, for God's sake. The binding is tightly cinched and held together with bits of leather strips and fringe. It looks like a saddle. My diary is also embossed, though not as discreetly as Madison's. Papa blowtorched my name into the cover. His calligraphy is absolutely beautiful, but the tool he used must have been pretty unwieldy because the letters are gigantic. As big as the cover is, and it takes up half the table, it still wasn't big enough to hold my name on one line. My diary says

SOPHIA

KAND

IN

SKY

which is kind of poetic and everything when you look at it from a certain angle. I keep trying to remind Papa that I now prefer to be called Sophie, not Sophia. I guess it's a little hard for him to remember, what with everything else he's trying to get used to and remember.

There are a lot of little things like that.

Every single sheet of paper in my diary is handmade. This means I have dark spotty beige pages, which are "beautifully textured," rather than snowy white smooth ones. The whole thing looks like it should be under glass somewhere. I've been sitting here for more than two hours trying to think of an appropriately momentous first entry.

Papa and Mama are both out and I'm alone, which is good. I simply can't write when there are people around.

And . . . apparently, I can't write when I'm alone either.

The darned thing is so big and stiff, I have to prop open the cover with my left shoulder and then try to hold the rest of it down with my right arm and the top of my chest.

I stare at the wavy, mottled paper.

I have writer's block.

Maybe a drink would unclog my writing pores, but I only drink when the Aunties sneak over plum brandy in Auntie Luba's all-purpose evening bag. Alcohol has not been allowed in any of our flats or apartments or this condo because Papa used to have liquor issues. Prison cured that. So, it wasn't all for nothing, as Auntie Eva likes to say on a fairly regular basis.

I suppose I could write about Papa coming home, but it's complicated. See, Mama and I had turned into pretty fair liars when it came to Papa. We had to. It was a survival thing. And last year, when I entered grade nine at Northern Heights Collegiate, we killed him. It was actually Papa's idea. It was supposed to be one of those "fresh start" deals. So Papa died of exploding arteries and I miraculously became friends with the Blondes.

It was all good.

It worked like a charm.

Except that it was finally proven that Papa didn't, in any way, slaughter the poor dead guy, which was better than brilliant except, except, here's the thing . . . Papa is *supposed to be dead*!

That's the complicated part.

Still, all in all, it's great. Papa is doing his best to wrap his head around the fact I'm not eight and, actually, he's doing better at that than Mama usually does. He can't stop looking at me and that's okay. Really. I get it. He's trying to catch up, and besides, Papa *really* sees me. Papa looks and sees his special Princess.

Mama looks and sees a work in progress.

Well, there's nothing to write about there.

A diary is supposed to be a repository of all your innermost secrets and thoughts—truthful ones.

I've been lying for so long, I'm not even sure I can do "truth" any more. Today, Papa answered the phone. We've been on him and on him about not doing that. So anyway, it was Kit, who naturally asked who the guy was.

So, naturally, I lied.

It was a pure knee-jerk lie. Without even pausing I heard myself say that it was my uncle, Papa's brother, who was going to be living with us for a while.

Shoot me now.

I can't keep up with myself.

I swear I've had it with the lying.

That's it!

Honesty.

What an excellent, thoughtful, very mature kind of self-improvement goal, a self-improvement goal anyone could be proud of. I picked up my pen.

It's September 1, 1975, and school starts tomorrow.

The paper was so "beautifully textured" that all the letters ended up crooked and blotchy. Papa was on an honesty kick too. Yesterday, he promised Mama that he would never, ever lie to her again. He promised while they were in the kitchen having a "moment." They hugged and Mama started crying. I could tell she believed him.

Which is good, I guess.

See, Papa never lied to me. He didn't have to. He loved me that much. That, and I was the keeper of all his secrets.

So, if Papa could promise to never lie to Mama again, I could maybe resolve to tell everyone the whole truth and break my lying cycle once and for all. For sure. What a relief! Absolutely.

Wait a minute.

There were complications.

Like I'm going to fess up to the entire student body that, stupendously, Sophie Kandinsky's father is alive after all. He's just been inconveniently locked up in the Kingston Penitentiary for seven years for something he didn't do but was too plastered to remember who did.

I think not.

Madison knew the whole deal, of course. It was her father and grandfather who helped get Papa out. Madison wouldn't be a problem either way. She had her own *complications*. But I had to tell the rest of them. Kit and Sarah deserved the truth. I trusted them. They were my friends, and friends tell each other the truth.

When they can.

Okay. I wrote very carefully, very truthfully.

> *I love Luke Pearson.*
> *Papa is finally, finally home and so far so good.*
> *I am going to tell the Blondes the truth.*
> *I will absolutely be more honest and*

Good, that looked good, but . . . uh, oh what the hell,

> *I still want to be a Blonde.*

Madison looked like she'd been caught red-handed smuggling nuclear weapons out of the country. As far as I could tell, she was only trying to hustle Edna Ryder out the door as she was trying to hustle me in. Edna wasn't having any of it.

"Sophie, honey, baby! How are ya, kid?" Edna gripped both my arms with a shocking amount of power, given that she couldn't weigh more than seventy-eight pounds. "Nice to see ya." *Prrrut.*

Did she just . . .? I looked at Madison, who looked at my shoes. I looked back at Edna, who rewarded me with a big gummy smile.

"I haven't seen enough of ya, if ya know what I mean. I'm always saying to my granddaughter here, bring that nice little Sophie over." *Prrrut.*

Was I the only one hearing this?

Edna patted her hair. "I mean, you're practically responsible for me having a granddaughter, know what I'm saying? What a word, eh? *Granddaughter.* I could say it over and over again. So, how's it going with your old man out of the Pen?" Madison winced each time the word *granddaughter* was mentioned.

I winced at the "out of the Pen" part.

"Good," I nodded. "Great even, all things considered. He's looking for a job at this very minute." At least, that's what I thought he was doing. When I left for my shift at Mike's restaurant that morning, Papa was at the kitchen table meticulously cutting out want ads from the *Toronto Star, The Globe and Mail,* and the *Toronto Sun.* It looked like he was contemplating something that would involve varnish and decoupage brushes. I would've thought that he'd just underline phone numbers and call people. But what do I know?

"I like your hair, Mrs. Ryder." It was hard not to notice that Edna had sort of permed her hair. It was still short and fluorescent yellow, but now her face was ringed with tight, furry little curls, while the back stood up in spiky random tufts.

"Thanks, doll, it's a Toni, know what I'm saying?" Edna patted her curls with pride. "Couldn't reach all the way back, but I always say it don't matter what people think of ya when you're leaving a room just when you're coming in, eh?" She winked. "I know you know what I'm saying." *Prrru . . .*

Okay, not as decisive as the last two times, but *that* was a fart. Edna was definitely farting up a storm. I didn't remember that about her. I'd last seen Edna at her apartment at the end of June, with Madison's family in tow. This was right after we had sorted out that Edna was indeed Madison's biological grandmother. Since this little bomb came right on the heels of Madison's finding out about my even bigger bomb—that Edna remembered me and Papa from her prison visits—I couldn't remember any of it without major-league cringing.

"You okay, sweet pea?" she asked.

"Yes, ma'am," I nodded. "It's really nice to see you again."

She gripped me tighter.

There was no getting around it: Edna so did not fit into the almighty, old-money perfection of the Chandler family portrait. Madison's grandfather, who owned the mansion they all lived in, was a judge and her parents were both professors, for God's sake. Edna, as far as we could figure out, was a career waitress at the Burger Inn.

"Edna was just leaving." Madison reached for the door.

"Yup . . . yup, yup, yup." *Prrrut.* "I just dropped in a sec to gaze at my miracle granddaughter, know what I mean?" She patted Madison's cheek.

Madison smiled, but she flinched on the inside. I felt it.

"Yup, yup," Edna said. "I know you girls have to work on that big physics laboratory thing. Physics," she snorted. "Girls today, I tell ya, know what I'm saying?"

Well, no, actually.

Edna was the only person I had ever met who could give my Aunties a race in the non sequitur sweepstakes. Besides, neither Madison nor I was taking physics. The plan was that we were just going to hang out for a while, since I couldn't go with the Blondes to Ginny Miller's "Back to School Bash" later that evening.

Madison's stare bored into me.

"Oh, God, yeah, it's this really complicated electronic biosphere particle sound thingy. It'll take forever to set up."

Okay, it was a lie but not really *my* lie, even though it came out of *my* mouth. It was a lie in defence of a friend in need's lie. This was definitely on Madison's back.

"What a world, know what I'm saying?" *Prrrrrut.* "Well, say hi to your old man, Sophie, and wish him luck at the job thing. It ain't easy for an ex-con out there."

Wince.

"Maybe I could put a word in for him at the Burger Inn."

Somehow I couldn't see it. "Thanks, Mrs. . . ."

She grabbed me again. "I keep telling ya, kid, it's just Edna."

"Thanks, Edna, I'll be sure to tell him." Madison was rolling her eyes.

"And, Madison, honey, I'm really looking forward to dinner next Sunday. You tell that little foreigner maid ya got that Gramma Edna is bringing her world-famous Hawaiian jellied marshmallow salad." One last stroke of Madison's cheek and she was gone.

Madison slumped down on the second step of the centre hall staircase. I slumped down beside her. "Well, she's unique," I said. "Uh, am I hearing right? Does Edna . . .?"

Madison sighed. "Apparently Edna has developed rather chronic gas issues."

"So, like, what, she's an uncontrollable farter?"

"Gas issues," Madison corrected. "It's a medical thing."

"Well, she really is trying and . . ."

"I don't want to talk about it. Let's go to my room. I bought at least a hundred pairs of stockings to go with my new mini."

Case closed. When most people say, "I don't want to talk about it," they, in fact, really do want to talk about it.

Not Madison. She shuts up tighter than a vault.

Each one of the beautiful pairs of pretty patterned pantyhose and coloured stockings was too small for Madison—the downside of being a blonde Amazon goddess. The crotch barely reached her mid-thigh. She'd have to settle for the old-lady nearly nude pair that her mother bought for her at the big and tall shop. I, on the other hand, was now the proud owner of six new pairs of baby blue and white stockings, plus three pairs of fishnets, all of which came up to my armpits.

"So, when are we going to tell them?" I asked.

"Tell who what?" Madison frowned at the mirror. "It's such a bummer that you're not coming. Ginny Miller always throws THE to-be-seen-at party of the fall term and you know how important it is that we make a statement as a group, especially at seniors' parties."

The Blondes and their Blonde rules.

"I know," I nodded. "But I have to be at home. It's a command performance. The Aunties are coming over en masse. Mama's been holding them off to give Papa some breathing room, but they couldn't be put off any longer. I have to referee. Papa and the Aunties have this mutual contempt thing going on." I tried on a pair of navy blue windowpane stockings. "And, oh yeah, by the way, Kit thinks that Papa is Papa's brother."

Madison raised an eyebrow.

"Don't ask."

She shrugged.

"Which brings us right back to . . . when are we going to tell them, Madison?"

She stepped out of nearly nude pantyhose and drop-kicked them into a corner.

"Madison."

"Well, I don't exactly remember agreeing that we'd tell them, exactly."

"Come off it, Madison, we've been talking about this for weeks." Or was that just me? "We need to tell them. I'm done with the lies. I've had it, you know? We need some help here."

Madison started trying on shoes. "Look, Sophie, I've known Kit and Sarah a lot longer than you have and I love 'em to pieces . . . well, thing is . . . I mean, Kit's been in California all summer with her mom and Sarah's been little miss camp counsellor, like, their lives are so . . ."

"Madison, you and I have been sitting on this powder keg for two months, and we've come up with nada, zilch, squat. As of last week, my father is his own brother. Like, how gross is that?"

"Papa? Oh, *your* stuff? Oh, absolutely, we've got to tell them about that. There's no way to keep your dad totally under wraps. We need them to help cover, if nothing else."

That was too easy.

She examined her legs. "Maybe I'll just Coppertone. I've done that before. Remember the Allen pool party? I can get it so it doesn't look too orange."

"You can't keep Edna under wraps forever either."

"I know."

"We could do it in one big swoop—like—look, guys, here's the thing: Sophie's dad is *not* dead and I *am* adopted.

Now the bad news, the dad was in prison all this time and my actual birth mother is dead. But, but, but . . . the good news is that the dad's been cleared thanks to Grandfather, and my ever-so-amusing new grandmother is actually a fabulous part of my life, all thanks to Sophie tracking her down last year."

"Uh, hmm." She had on one flat sandal and one high-heeled sandal. We went through this every time. Madison owns, like, a thousand pairs of heels, but she never wears them because she'd be taller than most of the football team in them. "Or something like that."

"Look, even I can tell that Edna's a tad, uh, especially for you guys, but she's kind of a riot, don't you think? If you look at it from a, uh . . ."

"I *know*, Sophie."

"Secrets eat you up, Madison. They change you." Jesus, I sounded like a hotline crisis counsellor.

She grabbed my arm. "I KNOW, Sophie."

Of course she did. Madison's been keeping her secret for a lot longer than I've been keeping mine. I had her.

Okay, well, so there you have it. I left with my toes freshly polished, six new pairs of stockings, and the certainty that we'd both finally come clean.

So . . . that was settled then.

God, I'm good.

It is always advisable to prepare oneself before entering the alternative universe of an Auntie visit. Sure, there are only three of them, but they can feel like a hockey team. Each Auntie had swooped in for individual reconnaissance visits over the past few weeks "Ven I just happened to, poof like magic, accidentally be finding myself in za neighbourhood of your lobby downstairs." Apparently, Auntie Eva, who drank like a fish, had grilled Papa on his drinking, Auntie Radmila, who had never worked a day in her life, had grilled Papa on future job prospects, and Auntie Luba just wanted to know if we were all crazy happy.

The Aunties were fanatically devoted to Mama and me. Each of them, including Mama, came from a different Eastern European country. Somehow, and I was still hazy on the details, they all met in Budapest. Since Mama was only in her teens, the Aunties became her de facto guardians and protectors, until Mama married and Papa mistakenly thought he was taking over. By the time I was four, we all found our way to Canada. Within a couple of years, given Papa's various, well, challenges, the Aunties became *my* de facto guardians.

And fabulously inappropriate ones at that.

Unlike Mama, who lived and died by my every report card, the Aunties displayed a commendable lack of interest in my school work. They just mainly wanted to know if I was having any fun yet. Until we moved here and I met the Blondes, things had been pretty grim on the fun front. The little I know about sex, I learned from the Aunties during our evenings of five-card stud while Mama was at night school or selling houses. My first taste of brandy, my first bra, and a barrage of glamour tips, like why it's important to daub perfume on the backs of your knees, were all doled out between sips of sweet Turkish coffee.

The Aunties would kill for either Mama or me, which was usually comforting, except that I suspected that they were in there sizing up Papa for his coffin. I reached for the door.

Papa and Auntie Eva were already squared off on either side of our newly purchased glass coffee table. Auntie Eva was pulsing like a strobe light. On top of the table was a huge cardboard carton. Auntie Radmila and Auntie Luba were sipping from their demitasse cups, enjoying the show immensely, while Mama paced with the coffee carafe in her hand.

Everyone turned to me.

"Hi, guys!"

We fixed our positions and went into the automatic Auntie Greeting Formula. Carved in granite, this was a ritual of rituals that I got better at with each passing year.

"SOPHIA! Buboola, beautiful angel!" Auntie Eva unclenched her fists and threw out her arms. "Come give kisses!"

"Oooo, look, she is getting fat! It's fantastic!" squealed Auntie Radmila.

"Da, da!" Auntie Luba clapped her hands. "Too, too beautiful!" I was smothered in a Luba hug. "I can't be standing it."

"Tanks be to God!" Auntie Eva ripped me from Auntie Luba. "It's a totally difference since za child got her period! Miss Canada vould looks like a lizard beside *our* Sophia. Vat a change, I should drop dead if I'm lying!"

I'd just seen them all three days ago at Auntie Luba's.

Mama looked pathetically relieved for the distraction.

"Well, you're all a sight for sore eyes too," I said as soon as the kissing, cheek squeezing, and hugging were over.

Vigorous "pshawing" and hand waving.

"No, I mean it."

Papa sat down and exhaled.

"Auntie Eva, is that a new hair colour?" She patted her champagne-coloured beehive. "It's fabulous, makes you look ten years younger. Auntie Radmila, you should wear *only* that sparkly green colour, and, Auntie Luba, my God, you're going to have to stop losing so much weight." I raised my finger for Auntie emphasis. "Too thin is too thin."

More "pshawing" mixed with nods of approval.

Not bad, if I do say so myself. They all sort of drank me in and beamed.

"So what's in the box, guys?"

Everyone stood up again.

"Ve have brought you a little gifts, some very excellent true to za life books." Auntie Eva glared at Papa. "Not just some fairy-airy poetry."

"Eva, I will not have that smut in my house!" Papa glared back.

Smut? Smut had my instant attention. They brought me smut? Wait till I tell the Blondes.

"Is not smut!" bellowed Auntie Eva. "You are a smut for calling za kettle black."

Well, we'd devolved into name-calling a little quicker than I had expected, although I could tell that Papa was still trying to decipher that last insult.

"Ziz books is about life! More life zan zat hair in za clouds poetry you make za poor child to reading." She reached into the box and brandished a pocket book with raised gold lettering: *The Flame and the Flower.*

Whoa! What a cover! My head was buzzing. I was mesmerized by all that embossed gold. I could only see a few of the books as I glanced into the box, but oh, what titles! *Office Love Affair, Call Her Savage, The Barbarian Lover, The Magnificent Courtesan,* and those were just the books on the very top! I wanted to be loyal to Papa. It wasn't a fair fight. Auntie Eva against anybody was immediately ten to one against the anybody. But I mean, *A Flame Too Hot*!

"I will not have her subjected to that trash! I want it out of the house."

Now wait just a darned minute here.

Auntie Luba swayed over to Papa and stroked his arm. "Trash? Is not trash, Slavko, I'm telling you true." She patted the box. "Zis is life, romance, love, hardship, and zen more love, and usually for sure maybe some kissing."

"It's trash fantasy. I can tell by the covers."

Oh, come on, the covers were better than chocolate.

Papa was waving around one called *Sweet Savage Love*. It had a glossy white cover with raised, shiny, brilliant blue lettering. A half-naked man was about to devour a woman with really long *curly* hair. The room disappeared.

"Everyting za child needs to know about life iz in zis book." Auntie Radmila snatched it from him and clutched it to her chest.

He was out of practice. It had been years after all. Papa had forgotten that he didn't stand a chance.

"It is NOT life! *Sweet Savage Love* my foot! It's a lousy, stinking romance novel. It NEVER happens." Papa snatched it back and tossed *my* book into *my* carton. "Magda." He turned to Mama. "You would never read such useless filth, would you?"

Mama had been shockingly silent thus far, mainly because she couldn't get a word in edgewise. "I—"

"She doesn't have to read a romance fantasy, Slavko," Auntie Eva pounced. "Her LIFE is a romance fantasy!"

Papa braced himself for the shot.

Then, like magic, Auntie Eva changed tack. She turned on a dime and smiled at Papa. "Slavko, my Slavko." I swear she was purring. "Vat is a romance novel but a beautiful voman is sweeping avay by a beautiful man. Zey are crazy in love togezer, ah?"

Well, that was Mama and Papa all right.

"Zen zer are many, many complications. People don't approve," she smiled. "Sound a little bit familiar, ah?"

She had him. On the one hand, Papa's parents, who were minor aristocrat types in Poland, thought Mama was a peasant. On the other, the Aunties all had an instant hate on for Papa.

"Za beautiful young lovers get married anyvay and stay in love no matter vat stupid bad tings happen." Auntie Eva raised an eyebrow. "Nobody can keep za young lovers apart and in za end, the prince finally comes home to his real estate qveen. Iz not life, Slavko? Magda does not have to be reading a romance novel. Magda's *life* is a big fat romance novel. I am resting on my cases." She sat back down and delicately patted her forehead with a lace hanky. No criminal lawyer could have delivered a more perfect or passionate summation.

Defeat was etched all over Papa's face. "Well, I want them kept in your room. I don't want to see those books anywhere else in our home."

"Yes, Papa, of course." I snatched the carton while the snatching was good and lugged it into my room, running my fingers over the lettering of *Sweet Savage Love,* just once, slowly, before returning to the living room.

When I got back, they were passing around kielbasa and pickled peppers and patting one another's thighs. The rest of the evening went shockingly well, given the combustibility of the dinner guests. Auntie Eva told one of her better stories about being "on za stage in Budapest," and Mama filled in everyone on the state of the Toronto real estate market. Papa was even cajoled and flattered into singing a couple of Polish folk songs. Auntie Eva was practically cooing at him, and she doesn't usually coo without several brandies.

The Aunties had done it.

They would continue to be welcome in my father's home. Oh, they still hated Papa, didn't trust him, forgave him nothing, I knew that. Papa probably knew it too. But the door would be open to them.

I had a lot to learn.

But I was learning from the best.

I stayed up most of Saturday night reading *Sweet Savage Love* and finished reading it by Sunday—a new Sophie Kandinsky reading record. The book weighs in at more than seven hundred pages of pure body-boggling, rapturous, sweaty, sin adventure. What a novel! Next, I gulped down *Cruise to a Wedding* (187 pages) and *The Flame and the Flower* (350 pages). Over the next few weeks I considered, and then put aside, all of the nurse romance books. It seems that I have no nurse or nurture impulses. I'd like to, but I don't, so there you go. I did, however, tear through *When Debbie Dared, One Tropical Night, Detour to Romance,* and *Lucifer's Angel.* Those impulses I got.

Then, I read *Sweet Savage Love* all over again. This time I highlighted all the really steamy bits, like the one on page 157: *"His hands moved slowly down the back of her neck, lifting the heavy coil of hair, and she trembled at the light, warmly caress-ing touch of his lips."* Now, that's what I call *writing*.

There were a lot of yellow highlighted bits in the story of the beautiful, *curly-haired*, quasi-aristocratic Ginny Brandon, and the mercurial, fantastically hunky Captain Steve Morgan. Somebody was either throbbing or pulsing, or both, on every page while galloping through several countries and getting mixed up in a handful of revolutionary wars.

I did my other stuff too, of course. I went to school and to basketball practice. We all made a "pity appearance" at gooey Jessica Sherman's birthday bash because, despite former bad blood between her troop and my Blondes, we were on the same basketball team after all. I did my homework, worked at Mike's on Saturday mornings, and kept an eye on Papa. But when I wasn't doing all of that, I was either rereading, high-lighting, or reciting entire passages of *Sweet Savage Love* to the Blondes. Ginny Brandon *was* me! Okay, so she had red hair and her father was a state senator, but it was *curly* red hair. Not only that, but she was feisty and spirited and didn't have much in the way of boobs.

I glanced over at my state senator. Papa was barely visible on the couch, smothered in falling-apart books and reams of paper. The sofa had become his "office" of choice over these past few weeks. It was Papa's goal to translate into English every single poem ever written in Polish. He was at the 1790s. Mama was at the kitchen table with me, sighing heavily and glaring at the living room as she thumbed through my test and essay results so far. I was desperate to get back to Ginny and Steve, who were waiting for me in my bedroom.

"Vell!" Deep sigh. "Dis grey skies is not going to clear up and put on a happy face." She was talking to me but eyeing the untouched weekend newspapers stacked by the television. Papa was definitely slowing down on the want-ads clip art project. "You vill be failing da algebra for sure if you are going to be so lazy and losing your brains to da smut books."

Well, at least they had found something to agree about.

I snatched the test out of her hands. "Mama, I got an eighty-seven, for God's sake!"

Mama snatched it back without breaking eye contact with the untouched newspapers. She got up, scraping the floor impressively with her chair, and jangled the keys to the Pink Panther. "Da goulash is in da oven. I got two houses to be showing tonight." She said the last line in her full big voice, so that the newspapers could hear her.

Papa turned a page and started scribbling in the margin.

Out again. This was not the way normal people lived. I was almost sure of it. "Mama, you're, like, never home." Somehow, the impossible had happened—there were times when I actually missed her.

She ignored me and grabbed her jacket. "Somevon," she said to the living room, "has to be vorking all of da times because to have money costs money. It does not grow vit da trees."

I chose not to unravel it. "Good luck."

The door slammed.

Papa flinched.

Well, all modern nuclear families have their little ups and downs.

I went to my bedroom and retrieved my handy-dandy diary from under my mattress and made a big show of lugging it into the kitchen. Papa picked up another tattered volume.

October 2, 1975

> *I'm going through a deeply invisible phase. This sucks. Ginny Brandon is "spirited" and is not invisible. I positively ooze "spirited" and yet . . .*

It was my first entry since my first entry and that was pretty much it. I was invisible.

It's not like anybody's mean or weird or anything. Me and the Blondes are tight, always together, but not really. Sort of like Mama, Papa, and me. Madison seems a bit floaty. She's probably figuring out how to let loose with her adoption bombshell. Kit's cool, except that she sounds like she swallowed a psychiatrist. Everything is either "really regressive" or "highly evolved" since her mom plunked her into some California teen therapy thing for kids who puke, which, naturally, is a secret. Even Sarah is more than her usual flaky, distracted self. And then there's Mama, who even when she's around, doesn't know I'm around.

It's not personal.

I'm pretty sure.

Some of my romance heroines would take to their beds after having something called the vapours. Okay, not Ginny, but lots of the other ones. They have this highly admired, highly sensitive, and highly strung nature that throws them into a life-threatening depression at the drop of a hat. Not only that, but they get a whack of attention for it. I considered having a depression. Actually, I'd been trying to put it into place for a few days.

I never had a depression before. I don't think. Even last year, when I tried to kill myself with five cherry-flavoured children's Tylenol, well, that was more panic than depression. It was the day Madison and I tracked down Edna, who recognized me from visiting Papa in prison. I wasn't even depressed then, just freaked out of my skull and demented—whole different thing—not useful here.

I could wear black, but it's really not a good colour choice for me.

I spent four whole periods on Wednesday sighing heavily from class to class.

Nobody noticed.

Even Luke. Hell, especially Luke. Not only was I invisible to him, but it looked like he was avoiding me. Had I misread every little thing from last year? It seemed that the only person I was not invisible to in the entire universe was his so-called girlfriend, Alison Hoover. Every time we came within hailing distance of each other, Alison made a huge, extravagant show of fingering a Northern senior class ring that was welded to a 24-karat-gold chain resting on her 36 double-Ds.

Luke's class ring.

She did it once when I was walking with Kit and I became visible long enough to have Kit whistle. "Whoa, that girl must be putting out at all hours and in all positions to have severed

Pearson's ring from his finger." Then she smacked my back. "She sure wants to make sure you see it though."

I needed one of those romantic, sensitive episodes where I don't get out of bed for days—like Mama used to do for all those years after a particularly bad prison phone call from Papa.

Yeah.

The Aunties would swoop in offering advice, and read me excerpts from *Sweet Savage Love* to keep my strength up. Papa would hover by the door, admitting that it was damn fine literature after all. Mama would drop everything and be inconsolable with guilt, which would in no way draw attention from me. She would stay home and, when she wasn't lovingly brushing the hair off my forehead, she would cook elaborate meals just for me. Or them—I'm not sure if depressives eat.

The Blondes would hold a bedside vigil, arguing about the relative benefits of Valium versus vodka while simultaneously apologizing for being so distracted by their own petty, pukey, little problems that they had totally lost sight of my fabulousness.

Who am I kidding? I suck at depression. I wrote down one of the highlighted bits from page 12: *"Ginny's spirits were too high for her to be able to contain them."*

Depression was simply not an option for people like us. But then again, neither was invisibility.

"Princessa." Papa was standing in front of the kitchen table, looking right at me. He "saw" me. I'd forgotten. Papa always saw me. "Princessa, enough writing for the both of us. How about a little treat before dinner?"

"Okay, Papa. Good idea." I could consider depression after ice cream.

Papa winked. He went and got the footstool from their bedroom and brought it back into the kitchen. Once in place, he stepped on it and then opened up the cupboard above the fridge. After rummaging around for a bit, Papa emerged holding a bottle of Five Star brandy. Further rummaging produced two shot glasses.

"Papa, you . . . I . . ."

He pressed his finger against his mouth. "Shhh . . . it will be our little secret, Princess."

"Uh, see the thing is . . ."

Papa glanced down at my diary.

I shut it and tried for a smile. "Diaries are supposed to be secret."

"Ah!" He winked. "I understand completely, a secret is a secret." He poured a finger of brandy into one of the shot glasses and handed it to me. Before I could protest, Papa put up his hand. "Princess, if I know your Aunties, this will not be your first brandy."

He had me, had us. The Aunties had been sneaking me the occasional shot for years. He poured the second shot to the brim of the glass, like Auntie Eva always did.

"But, Papa, don't you think . . . I mean, Mama doesn't . . ."

"Never mind Mama for the moment." He raised his finger to his lip. "I've got the inside track on some incredible opportunities and then Mama will be back to her best self."

"Yeah. But, Papa, the thing is . . ."

"I can handle your mother, Princess." He winked. "Salute!"

Clearly, his years of incarceration had dulled what should have been an appropriate fear of Mama. "But . . ."

"Sophia, heart of mine, a man needs to be a man."

I nodded. I didn't know how sneaking a drink made anybody more of a man exactly, but we clinked glasses. It was naughty and secretive and, and, well, fun, like all those years ago. Just the two of us, before Papa went away.

"You were looking so lost." He downed half his glass. "This is very difficult, the situation. You are just a child—a beautiful child, but a child still. And all of this," he sighed and waved his hand around in the air, "it's not fair to you. But, Princess, I promise that I'm going to make it work because you deserve it."

Papa topped up his drink and then put the bottle right back into its hiding place. There. That's what was different. Papa had only had a couple of drinks.

Well, one and a half really.

And I had had one with him. So, it was completely different.

I nodded. "I know you will, Papa."

He winked again as he downed the brandy. "And this will be our little secret, Princess?"

"Sure, yeah, Papa." I downed my brandy in one warm golden gulp.

Yup, definitely different.

We were all at Kit's celebrating the fact that her dad was out of town at a dentist convention. Mr. and Mrs. Cormier were finally and officially separated. In what was, at least to me and the Aunties, a mind-boggling concept, it was *Mrs.* Cormier who took off. She had to "find herself." Apparently she had to go all the way to California to start looking. It was my first taste of "Blonde complexity." Anyway, all of us really liked poor Mr. Cormier and we weren't going to blow his trust in us by having some gross, out-of-control drunk with half the school trashing the place.

We were going to handle it very maturely.

It would just be us doing the drinking.

Madison and I agreed that this would be as good a time as any to come totally clean. We agreed on the phone at precisely 4:47 that afternoon. By 7:22 P.M. that night, I was seriously regretting it.

"What the hell!" Kit strode menacingly toward me. Well, as menacingly as anyone could with cotton balls tucked in between her toes. "Let me get this straight! You're telling me that your uncle is your father? Let's leave aside that there are probably laws about things like that *and* that it's too creepy for words, but this uncle/father person is the same dad who dropped dead from some kind of artery explosion seven years ago?"

I may have nodded.

"And, *and* . . . Madison has known about this whole deal the whole damn summer!!!"

Sarah threw her arm around me. "Poor Soph."

"Poor Soph, my ass!" Kit threatened me with a nail polish brush. "She LIED to us! And not only that, even when Madison found out, she kept on lying to you and me, Sarah. I mean, holy . . ."

I cocked my head toward Madison. She should jump in here. Yup, this would be a good spot. Instead, Madison continued to apply, remove, and then reapply nail polish. She seemed to be torn between Cherries in the Snow and Sweet Pretty Pink.

"No, no, no, it wasn't like that." Okay, that came out whinier than I would've liked. "Remember, it was Madison's grandfather who found out. He put two and two together way back last year, but he didn't, uh . . ."

Jesus, I couldn't talk about Edna's role in all of this until Madison coughed up her bit.

I screamed telepathic messages at Madison: *Now! Tell them now, Madison!*

She reached for more nail polish remover.

"Yeah, well, then, all of a sudden, the Judge and Madison's father started the whole wheel of justice thing steamrolling and, presto, got Papa out."

"Whoa." Kit turned to Madison. "I thought that your gramps was kinda sweet on Sophie's WIDOWED mother. And now he's responsible for unwidowing her. Bummer."

"Yeah," we all said, even me.

"All right then," said Sarah. "Let's recap, shall we? Sophie's father is not dead."

We nodded.

"Sophie's father was unjustly, um, incarcerated for years for something he didn't do and our Sophie . . . ," she threw her arm around me again, "has had to endure years of abject abuse and serial school changing, as a result of this initial tragic injustice."

I looked at Sarah as if I'd never seen her before. Clearly all that blonde hair had distracted me from realizing just how smart and sensitive she was.

"Of course she had to lie about him." Sarah hugged me, again.

"Yeah, yeah, yeah," grunted Kit. She glanced at Madison. "Madison, whoa, step away from the nail polish remover, girl. You'll be down to the nubs on your next redo."

Madison drew herself up. She finally seemed to remember herself *and* her station in our natural pecking order. She didn't say anything though.

"But, but the important thing is that Sophie's father is alive and well and is, at this moment, her uncle." Sarah shook her head. "We live in confusing times."

She had that right.

Were we actually talking about me? Me? It was like I was watching a movie about Blonde girls talking about their crazy friend who has this crazy father . . .

"Thing is," Sarah plugged on. "We have to watch our Sophie's back on this. If this hits the school, it could be, well, awkward."

"Speaking of back watching." I raised my eyebrows at Madison.

She actually smiled at me before she looked away.

Kit kicked over the ottoman. "Damn it, Soph! You could've told me. I would've got it!"

"I know, I know." I was mumbling. "It was like a disease. I swear, most of the time I believed me myself." I stepped toward her. She stepped back. "I know I should have told you, Kit. You would have gotten it, you especially."

"Hello, yoo-hoo!" Sarah waved her arms. "I'm the one who's being all supportive here."

Kit kicked the ottoman back upright and plopped down on it. "So, like, how weird is it at your house?"

"Pretty weird." Enough was enough, I walked over to Madison. We'd made a pact: I'd go, then she'd go. We'd share the load.

"Well, you can just imagine, Papa out of prison and all of us getting, uh, used to . . . ," I sat down beside her. "But the thing is, it's, uh, got to be weird at Madison's too."

"Yeah, how so?" Kit got up and grabbed a bottle of Southern Comfort and some 7UP.

Madison put down all her tools and started patting my knee.

Fasten your seat belts.

"Well, sure," Madison sighed. "What drama. Grandfather and Father working all their free time, calling in favours to get things 'expedited.'" She paused. "Are you going to get glasses and ice or are we chugging out of the bottle?" Kit and Sarah ran off to forage.

"Madison!" I whispered. "Madison, what the . . .?"

She crumpled and shook her head. Just as we heard them approach, she mouthed, "I can't."

And then, presto, she turned into Madison again. "Anyway, as I was saying, it was non-stop drama all summer, but so exciting too."

Can't? Right, so there you have it. I was left at the altar.

"Wow, yeah." Kit was shaking her head. "Your whole family was, like, this big knight in shining armour."

Madison shrugged prettily.

"How incredibly generous of them," said Sarah.

Great, now I was a charity case *and* a liar. I had tracked down her family for God's sake, her *real* family. I did it for her!

"Bluebloods with heart." Kit poured exactly one inch of Southern Comfort into each glass. "Wouldn't expect anything else from you, Madison. Hell, that's why you're you."

Yes sir. And who was that exactly?

Kit squirted some water back into the bottle and held it up to the light. "I think that's it for this bottle, guys, it's getting too light looking. I'll get the cherry brandy next."

"How'd they get him off?" asked Sarah, before she burped.

"It was almost too easy, really," said Madison. "Daddy got the bartender to sign an affidavit stating that Mr. Kandinsky had been entirely incapacitated way before the fighting even started. Apparently, the bartender had been double-crossed by the thugs who actually did it, so he was more than happy to cooperate."

"Expedited? Affidavits?" said Sarah. "You sound like your dad."

"*Blood* will tell." I raised my glass to her and gulped. I wasn't even going to drink. I only liked my ritual shot with the Aunties. I actually didn't much see the point of the whole getting drunk thing. I gulped again.

Madison shook her head. "So, since it could be proved that Sophie's father was, uh . . ."

"Passed out," said Kit.

"Indisposed," said Madison, "naturally, the Crown's case was in shreds and all that was left was the paperwork."

Shreds. I took another swig and dove back into that almost comfortable place where we were watching that nice movie about the nice Blonde girls discussing their nice but crazy friend's crazy life.

Out came the 7UP and cherry brandy.

"Your poor dad," said Sarah. "Like, how much does that suck?"

I was, for sure, loving Sarah more every minute.

"So, *is* your old man a drunk?" asked Kit, pouring herself another drink.

"Was a drunk," I said a bit drunkenly. "Prison, you know." We all nodded.

"But he's a poet, right, Sophie?" said Madison.

She was sucking up. It didn't help. I finished my drink. "Yeah, he's a poet and a freelance translator," I finally said.

"Cool," Sarah hiccupped.

Kit nodded thoughtfully. "So, like, people get paid for that?" It may have been the drink, but I thought she was sounding less belligerent.

"Well." I narrowed my eyes. They were all sort of turning into one big Blonde. "As you can imagine, it's very difficult getting re-established, what with the market and all." I didn't know what that meant, but it was word for word what Papa kept telling Mama.

"Well, the whole thing is straight out of one of your romance novels," slurred Sarah.

"To no more secrets!" I raised my glass.

"To no more secrets!"

Madison was the first one to clink me.

"Okay, okay." Kit put her hand up. "Now, cut it out before we all throw our arms around each other and start singing 'Kumbaya.'"

I laughed, but I didn't get it. That happened a lot. I wouldn't get it because it was about something that had taken place five years ago or it was a Blonde reference. They spoke in a code that involved summer cottages, black diamond ski runs, and Bloomingdale's. Sometimes I asked, but then I didn't get the explanations either. So, usually, if they laughed, I laughed.

We spent the rest of the evening in a warm, giggly bubble. I think we decided that we'd continue with the uncle scenario, which had the same-last-name bonus going for it. At some point, Madison helpfully proposed that in a year or so, Mama could actually marry my "uncle," because surely that kind of thing must happen in "the old country" all the time. We all

agreed that this seemed to be an eminently reasonable solution. Then Sarah promptly fell asleep on the record player.
The rest of us hit various parts of the floor shortly after.

At around 3:30, I felt my way to the bathroom.

It was occupied.

My stomach clenched. I had an instant flashback to almost
the same time, same place, and same situation last year.

I could tell it was Kit barfing. The door opened very
slowly. Her eyes were swollen slits.

"That you, Soph? Ow, my head . . . well, here we are in
the can again, ow, just like old times, eh?"

The hall and I were spinning in different directions. "Kit!
Were you puking? Jesus God. You were puking! How could
you?"

She leaned into the door jamb and held on to it for dear
life. She looked like she was trying to hold up the house.

"Oh, hose yourself down. Yeah, I was puking because of
the goddamned cherry, ow, brandy. I swear some words hurt
more than others. Do you have to puke?"

I shook my head and regretted it immediately, the head
shaking I mean. I never throw up. It's a thing—not with the
worst stomach flu, not with fevers—never. I had to wait for
the room to stop throbbing before I could speak. "Promise?"

"Hell, yeah, that was my third trip. I'm not doing this
again, ow. Let's face it, I've had enough barfing to last me a
lifetime." She let go of the door jamb long enough to try to
fold her arms, thought better of it, and reached for the door
again. "It hurt, man."

"Well, when you drink three cherry brandies and a—"

"You could have told me. You knew all my stuff, even about my fabulous summer in the clinic for head cases." She shut her eyes. "I have to see someone here too, you know."

I opened my mouth to say something profound. Nothing came out.

"Yeah, it's a real condition with a fancy name." She paused. "That I've forgotten for the moment. But I'm, like, over it now. Yeah, and, well, you just should have told me."

"I know." I grabbed hold of the other side of the door jamb to make it stop moving. "I know, Kit, I blew it, I, I . . . won't lie to you again."

"S'okay," she burped. "Man, you look like crap."

I was forgiven.

"You don't look so hot yourself."

"I think we better load up on some Bromo-Seltzer."

I started following her to the kitchen.

Then Kit stopped and turned so suddenly, I almost crashed into her. "One little thing though, Soph."

"Yeah?"

"Maybe I'm still drunk or something, but I have this feeling you're still holding back."

No, no, just Madison's adoption, her brand new grandmother, the part I played in all of that.

Kit looked at me. "Sophie?"

No more lies.

"Soph?"

I can't. "There's nothing, Kit."

She looked confused.

"You and me . . . we're clean. I promise."

"Okay." She turned on the lights in the kitchen, much too painful. She turned them all off again. "Okay, it's enough for me."

I could barely make her out in the dark.

"I believe you, Sophie."

I turned right back around.

"Hey, where are you going?"

The walls were pulsing again, and I was pulsing with them. "I'll be back in a minute. I think I'm going to be sick."

"It happens," she said.

6

I was trying to cultivate "stillness." It was a whole new strategy because the "spirited" thing wasn't working as effectively for me as it did for Ginny Brandon. The problem is that it takes a lot of energy for me to be still. Still, being "still" is "blonder" and thus, well, better. There we all were, Papa, Madison, Kit, and Sarah, in the corner booth at Fran's, and I was struggling to out-still the lot of them. We were having dinner to celebrate our first away game at Jarvis Collegiate. It was a pity party.

We lost. Big.

The good news was that all of us, including Jessica Sherman and Elaine Sawchuck from last year's Junior City Championship team, were recruited to the senior team. The bad news was that, aside from Elaine and beans-for-brains Jessica, there were pretty well no other seniors on our senior team. Mr. Wymeran, our nervous little coach, kept twittering about how "we are building, building, ladies!" So far, "building" meant that the other teams, who were more reasonably populated with older, heavier, and meaner girls, used us as rags to mop their floors.

Despite being beaten to a pulp, I was having difficulty with the "still" thing. What would they think of him? What would he think of them? Most important, what would everyone think of me as a result of all of this thinking? I mean, here we were sitting around and having burgers with my *lie*. I felt like I was vibrating.

Papa and the Blondes were having a happy little chat about the poetry evident in the game of basketball. True, Sarah kept trying to steer the conversation back to how many times she had seen *The Longest Yard,* but Papa gently explained that, as a rule, they didn't show prison movies in prison. They all talked, giggled, and asked questions. I bopped around, fidgeted with my fries, jumped up to bring the ketchup from the waitress station when she didn't bring it fast enough, mopped up Kit's cola ring, and rearranged the condiments until Kit grabbed my arm and whispered, "Chill, will ya? It's not Mike's, you're not working."

At least she thought it was waitress envy.

Papa insisted from the outset that dinner was on him. "It is my privilege to provide nourishment to such beautiful and clearly talented young athletes." He followed up with his best boyish smile, flashing both dimples, and brushed the hair out of his eyes. They didn't stand a chance. Meanwhile, I was having palpitations worrying about how we were going to pay for it, and where did he get the money, and did Mama give him an allowance, and Jesus, how humiliating was that? I started mopping up cola rings again.

Madison started to protest, but Papa raised his hand. "And . . . to help me celebrate my new job in journalism."

"Way cool, Mr. Kandinsky, congrats!" said Kit.

"That's so exciting, Mr. K.," heaved Sarah. "Wow, you must be so, so talented."

Papa rewarded her with a shy smile. "It's just part-time, really."

"But still!" they all said at once.

Truth is, calling it part-time was seriously stretching it. Papa was going to work every other Friday from 2:00 P.M. to 5:30 P.M. compiling local charity events and deaths for the community newspaper. He wouldn't even get a byline unless someone dropped dead during a strawberry social and he was on the desk at the time. As it stood, last week's cheque wouldn't cover the Coca-Cola bill.

But that didn't matter now. They loved him. He had them from "hello" back in the parking lot during the introductions. He had them from his handshake, by guessing who was who, and by observing one small, perfect thing about how each of them had played.

Madison laughed prettily at something Papa said. Even when she was laughing, Madison was serene. I used to believe that holding in a huge secret or lying changed you, especially if you held it in for a long time. I believed this because Sister Christina, four schools back, at St. Stephen's, said so. For years I'd stare at myself in the bathroom mirror looking for the deformed bits to start creeping in.

On bad days, I saw them.

I kept sneaking looks at Madison. She should look like the Hunchback of Notre Dame by now. Instead, Madison was beautiful and *still*. I was fighting a losing battle trying to stop myself from shredding everyone's paper napkins, when I heard a sharp, but dainty, intake of breath from Madison. Her eyes bulged out at me and she started brushing away imaginary crumbs from her chest.

I bulged right back at her with one eyebrow up, one down, which, of course, was the universal sign for "What the hell?"

She saw my signal and raised it with a direct glare at my breasts. Okay, so my shirt was covered in lemon meringue pie crust crumbs but . . .

"Why, Luke!" she said. "What on earth brings you to this neck of the woods?"

Luke? Jesus God. Did she say Luke? I started swatting at my chest in a panicked bid to remove the crumbs and bat the girls into growing instantly. It must've looked like I was trying to put out a fire.

"Madison, hey!" Luke moved to the side of the table. "And Kit and Sarah." Then he turned. "And . . . Sophie!"

There was a pause. Surely everyone caught it. A pause and, just for me, a great big smile. Jesus, what a smile, what teeth, what lips, what . . .

Luke reached over the table extending his hand to Papa. "Luke Pearson, sir. I go to school with these wild women."

Papa smiled and shook hands, but didn't say anything. It was like someone had thrown a blanket over the table.

Right.

We hadn't told Papa what our plan was for him. Papa was lost. Who was he supposed to be? By the look on Kit's and Sarah's faces, I could tell that they were cranking through a cherry brandy haze trying to remember *what exactly* it was we had decided as a plan.

"Mr. Kandinsky is Sophie's uncle from Cleveland who's been transferred to Toronto for his journalism career," said Madison without blinking.

Cleveland? The "transferred" was a nice touch though.

"Nice to meet any member of Sophie's family, sir." Their hands were still clasped, hard. Guys do this stuff so differently.

"The pleasure is entirely mine," said Papa.

Smooth, man, he was smooth. Did he learn this kind of thing in prison or was he always like that? I exhaled.

"We just got our asses—" Kit's hand shot to her mouth. "Sorry, Mr. Kandinsky. We just got cleaned by Jarvis."

Luke shook his head. "It's nothing." He turned to me again. "Hey, for a senior team you guys are babies. You're all punching over your weight for starters. It'll probably take you most of the season just to figure out the shot differential, but you girls are champions, don't ever forget that."

We would have five children, three boys, two girls. Luke Jr., Slavko Jr., Adam, and . . .

Luke put one hand at the back of my chair. "I'm on a mercy mission for my mom." He leaned in a bit. "Her book club is at our house and she forgot to pick up dessert, so I'm supposed to grab two coconut cream pies and save the day."

Wow, people "picked up" dessert rather than made it themselves? Papa and I both took a minute to digest this concept.

"I can recommend the lemon meringue," I finally said, sort of. Out of nowhere my mouth had turned into the Sahara Desert. I was salivaless, *sans* spit. Luke's mouth curved into a little half smile, just enough to let his dimple come out. He reached over and brushed a stray crumb off of my left shoulder. Oh God, we were going straight for a page 372! *"She could almost feel, like a physical thing, the burning gaze of his eyes on her face, her lips, her shoulders and . . ."*

"Okay then, one coconut cream and one lemon meringue it is." Luke brushed off another crumb. "Thanks for the tip, Sophie."

I drew myself up, tossed my head just so, and said, "Wrgagupplerr dithrptt."

Real words would have been so much better.

For some reason, Luke didn't seem to notice. "Well, it was, uh, great to see you guys, and to meet you, Mr. Kandinsky." Then he turned back to me, me, me. "Catch ya later, Sophie."

"Bye." We all waved our fingers and then held our breaths until Luke Pearson actually left the restaurant. Then we all exhaled at once.

"Whoa, Soph!" snorted Kit. "We weren't even in the room! Did you see that!"

"I got to hand it to you, Sophie, Lucas Pearson is one luscious-looking guy," sighed Sarah.

"Why are we handing anything to Sophia?" asked Papa. "Who is this boy? Do you like him, Sophia?"

Eew, eew, eew, gross. We were talking about my romantic life with my father!

Madison was right on it. "I am so sorry about the uncle thing, Mr. Kandinsky. See, we sort of decided that maybe the best thing for the, uh, foreseeable future, since you're supposed to, uh, have been, uh . . ."

"Dead?" nodded Papa. "No, it was, I understand completely." His eyes clouded. "It is a very awkward situation and your solution, ladies, is, was . . . inspired. I am very grateful that my Princess has such truly fine friends."

I watched them melt.

We drove everyone home in the Pink Panther, our 1969 candy-floss pink Buick Oldsmobile. Mama had risen so far in the realtor ranks that she got to use the company car when she had "important" showings, and Papa and I had the Pink Panther to ourselves. I can only assume that the company car is some hyper-tasteful shade of grey. Mama had a lot of important showings lately. She hadn't come to a single basketball practice or any of our games so far.

Not that I cared. It was a relief really. She always used to turn up at games, and even practices, cheering and hollering. It was excruciating, especially since Mama didn't know the first thing about basketball and the refs hated her. She was always screaming out perfectly useless movie quotes to *inspire* us. Like, out of nowhere, during a foul shot, you'd hear, "Dis von is for da Gipper!" Then I'd have to explain to Madison or whoever was taking the shot, "1940s college football movie, the Gipper is some dying, but great, player." And then the shot would be taken.

So, it *was* a relief. Mainly.

Papa at least knew the game. He fell in love with it the moment he landed in Canada. Auntie Eva liked to cite this as yet another example of Papa's pigheadedness. When every other self-respecting immigrant, including two of her former husbands, rightfully and immediately embraced the Canadian religion of hockey, Papa decided to worship basketball. And I, of course, worshipped it right alongside him.

"So, who is this Luke, Sophia?"

We were walking over to the condo.

"No one." I shrugged. "He's just a guy at school and he comes into Mike's every Saturday with the rest of the football team after practice."

Papa stepped in front of me and grabbed my shoulders. "Don't do that, Sophia. Don't. They took away my freedom, not my brains."

My heart pounded in my ears. He'd never done anything like that. "I'm sorry, Papa." My voice broke. "And I'm sorry about the uncle thing too. I, we just didn't know what to do, how to explain . . ."

He loosened his grip.

"And, Papa, I know there's so much to be said, should be said, to catch up on. All those years in prison, I want to know what you went through, I . . ."

"No." Papa drew me into him and kissed the top of my head. "We won't talk about any of that, ever. I don't want you to think about it, any of it. I will not have any of those kinds of pictures inside you. We Kandinskys do not look back. The only thing that matters is today. But the boy . . . ," he let go of me, "the boy likes you, and more important, I can tell you like him."

"No, Papa." It looked like he was going to grab me again. "I mean, I do, but he's been going steady with this, uh, girl, Alison Hoover, for almost two years and so he, the thing is, she's . . ."

Okay, how do you tell your father that the love of your life has been trapped by non-stop sexual gratification?

You don't.

"I see."

And yet.

He did.

"You'll have him."

"God, Papa," I moaned. "You sound exactly like Auntie Eva."

"Well, that would be a first," he smiled. "But for once that crazy old turkey is right. Sophia, this is difficult for a father, especially for a father who has missed so much of his daughter's life. But I won't miss one thing more. Not one. Don't shut me out of any of it." He looked at me hard. "Well, at least, as much as any young beautiful woman can share with her somewhat out-of-touch and confused Papa. Please, Sophia?"

"I promise, Papa."

He threw his arm around me and we walked across the street. "It pains me to say it, Sophia, but the boy is crazy for you."

"Yeah, right." I groaned.

"You'll see." He laughed.

"No way."

"Oh yes."

We went back and forth like that all the way to the condo, Papa's arm wrapped tightly around me. And despite our bickering, and despite the fact that we were taking gigantic Papa strides, for the first time in almost forever— I was still.

Sarah's family was spilling out of her house just as we were coming up the path. It was a five-bedroom Southern Gothic special. I know from houses. Two years ago, I spent months prepping Mama for her real estate exams. Kit lived in a sleek, modern, four-bedroom backsplit, all killer edges and earth tones. Madison rambled around in a turn-of-the-century Tudor mansion, and Sarah lived in this Canadian version of a plantation house, complete with Doric columns and shutters. A study should be done on this sort of thing. Each house suited each girl's personality perfectly. It was freaky.

It was also depressing. What did a two-bedroom, barely furnished condominium say about me?

Sarah's sisters, Susie, twelve, Shelley, nine, and Sally, seven, were all wearing these bizarre little brown or blue uniforms.

They kept zipping in and out of the house and around Sarah's extremely pregnant mother.

"Hi, Mrs. Davis," I shouted.

She was trying to stuff the girls into the family station wagon. She'd get the lagging Sally into one car door and then either Shelley or Susie would escape out the other. There were panicked shrieks about forgetting a Barbie or a juice box and then a tickle fight would break out. Through all this, Mrs. Davis didn't have a nuclear meltdown or even raise her voice. Instead, she sauntered over to us. "Sophie, dear, how nice to see you again." Shelley returned with an armload of Barbies and got into the car. "I can't tell you how relieved Bob and I are that you're in so many of Sarah's classes this year. She kept telling us all last year what a genius you are."

"Oh, I'm certainly not . . ."

Susie whipped by me carting three juice boxes and a bag of Cheezies.

"Nonsense, dear," she smiled warmly. "If Sarah says you're a genius, you're a genius." Mrs. Davis carefully folded herself into the driver's seat. "Okay, dear ones, off to Brownies and Guides, and then a quick Brown Owls meeting afterward."

"Is Maria making dinner?" asked Sarah.

"Darling, Maria left two weeks ago. The new maid is Julia, remember?" Mrs. Davis shut the door and rolled down the window. "And . . . I think Julia has the day off or . . .," she frowned, "or she quit. I can't quite remember which. It's been that kind of day. Not to worry, I'll pick up something. You're staying for dinner, Sophie. I'll figure it out by then." She smiled. "Give us a kiss, baby."

Sarah leaned her head into the car and planted a kiss on her mom. And somehow, without a shot being fired, everyone was in the car singing campfire songs and heading down the road.

Brown Owl?

Sarah slid her arm through mine. "I made a lemon poppy-seed cake yesterday. Want some?"

"You bet," I said. The chaos outside was mirrored by the chaos inside. Fisher-Price tricycles, kitchenette sets, and stuffed toys dotted the huge centre hallway as well as the living and dining rooms. The kitchen was a mess, not a dirty mess, just a wreck mess. Opened boxes of cereals and cookies commingled with an elaborate plastic tea party set in the middle of the counter. Mama would have been spastic with rage. I was a little uncomfortable myself.

Jesus, I was turning into my mother!

"Sit down and give your brain a rest while I get the cake."

A massive pine kitchen table was completely covered by Halloween craft projects. I had to move opened jars of white glue and orange glitter just to sit down. Sarah expertly manoeuvred around the obstacles, preparing the coffee, slicing the cake, and presenting it all perfectly.

"You actually made this?" I said, biting into a luscious lemony cake.

"Yeah," she frowned. "But the next time, instead of the lemon icing, which is too predictable, I think I'll do a chocolate ganache."

"You're the genius, Sarah."

"Oh, get off it." But she cut me another, larger piece.

"And it's you who makes those amazing brownies that you bring to practice, isn't it?"

She shrugged.

"Jesus, Sarah, you have a calling."

"Stop." She was actually blushing.

"No, I mean it. You could open your own restaurant, Sweet Sarah's, and only the really beautiful people would come."

Now she was red all over. "Thanks for that. You sound like my dad, but I couldn't do anything like that. I'm not like you guys. You're all going to end up being doctors and lawyers and diplomats."

"Oh, come on, that's just so . . ." Well, actually, I hadn't given it much thought, but I guess it sort of made sense. "You could do . . ."

She raised her hand. "No, really, I'm not like you guys. I don't want to run the world. I know my limits, okay? *My* dream is to have a whole pile of kids and a great husband, make brilliant meals for my family, and . . .," she shrugged again, "and maybe take everyone to Brownie meetings."

"Like your mom," I said.

"Yeah, except for the brilliant family dinners part."

"Wow."

"I knew you'd be disappointed."

"No, no, it's not that, I'm just trying to wrap my head around the idea that someone wants to be like their mother."

"Sophie Kandinsky, your mother is amazing!"

"*My* mother, unlike *your* mother, Sarah, is a hurricane who thinks I'm a complete failure unless I score a ninety in everything."

Sarah reached over to me. "She just wants for you what she didn't have for herself. It's quite typical of immigrant . . ."

"Oh, don't go all guidance counsellor on me. It's not even that, hell, I'm used to it, but she could cut Papa a little slack, you know? She's on him like a ton of bricks. The guy's been locked up for seven years. It's going to take more than a minute to get going and everything, right?"

I waited for some Papa sympathy.

Sarah nodded but she didn't say anything.

"And now all of a sudden she is super-career-woman, working all the time. Have you noticed she hasn't turned up to a single game, not that I care."

"Yeah, I miss her too. She was such a riot."

That was sooo not what I meant. What did I mean? "Okay, well then, we, uh, had better get on to the mysteries of the periodic table, eh?"

"Sure." Sarah bounced up. "Okay, let's go to my room. There's actually room in my room."

She was right. It was always the same: while the rest of the house looked like an upscale lost and found depot, Sarah's room was a sanctuary, immaculate and warm, cuddled in creamy white and blues.

I never wanted to leave.

After a gruelling grilling for more than an hour, I think I had her to an almost pass on tomorrow's test. We decided to celebrate with a facial before dinner. Sarah didn't have the stash of fabulous Christian Dior and Yardley beauty products that lined Madison's war chest, nor did she have the extensive, if motley, collection we had at our house, left over from

Mama's Mary Kay selling days. Sarah *made* her own beauty products. Rich people can be stupefying. Down we went to the kitchen again. I helped her whip up oatmeal, egg whites, lemon, and honey in a blender while she rhymed off the beautifying properties of each ingredient.

"Sarah, how can you possibly know all this and still flunk chemistry?"

"Shhh," she said while she smeared goop all over my face with a wooden spatula. "I've got to warn you, this goes rock hard in about twenty minutes. Now do me."

My face tingled.

"Now we'll slice some cucumbers and place them on our eyes while we put our feet up."

Well, fine, when in Rome . . . We went to lie down on the living room rug and put our feet up on the sofa cushions. This just so wouldn't happen at anyone else's house, including mine.

"Now think sexy thoughts," she instructed.

I was too embarrassed to admit that those were pretty well the only kinds of thoughts I'd been having lately. "Okay, I'll try, but . . . speaking of which, you never really told me about camp this year and how it was being a counsellor and, well, everything."

"Ahhh." I swear she growled. "It was brilliant."

My antennae went up. "Sarah . . . that guy from last year, the counsellor, Andrew was it? The one you almost, uh, was he there too?"

"Uhhmmmnnn." She was definitely growling, or purring. "Yup, Andrew was a junior director this year."

"Sarah . . ."

"Sophie . . ."

There was just something new in her voice, something . . .

"Sarah, Jesus God, you didn't!" I whipped off my cucumbers.

"Oh, didn't I?" Her cucumbers fell off. She tried to smile but the oatmeal was having none of it.

"Ohmygod, ohmygod, ohmygod!" She did, she did, she did! "You did?! You didn't! You did? Are you going to marry him? Are you sure you did IT? Do Kit and Madison know?"

"Yes, *nooo,* yes, and nooo! And don't you dare tell them. This has GOT to be our secret."

"But they're your best friends, Sarah." It was hard to whip up an earnest expression with concrete oatmeal on your face.

"And they're practically frigid. They won't get it."

"Sarah, Jesus, Kit spelled out her name in hickeys on Rick Metcalf's stomach last year. I mean . . ."

"That was just for show. Kit is an absolute prude." Sarah plopped onto the sofa. "I find it deeply ironic that here we are in the middle of the sexual and feminist revolution and my university-bound friends will probably remain virgins until their wedding day, while poor, intellectually challenged, homemaker Sarah is on the frontlines of the revolution."

"Hey, hang on to your pants a minute, I'm more frigid than anybody. You were there at that party when I practically castrated Ferguson Engelhardt for trying to feel me up."

"You're selective, Sophie," she sniffed. "It's not the same thing as being frigid. You're, like, obsessed with *Sweet Savage Love,* which I bought last week by the way, AMAZING book, and don't think I didn't see your body melt when Luke just touched your shoulder at the restaurant."

My face heated up. I was in danger of cooking the oatmeal.

"It's okay, Sophie, we're lusty girls. There's nothing wrong with that."

We?

Lusty?

Me?

Okay, so I did have this recurring fantasy about how I'm a voluptuous secret service agent and I have different lovers in all my ports of call. There is Eduardo panting for me in Rome. Eduardo is a sophisticated man of the world who is reduced to primitive animal desires whenever I enter the room. Then there's Jean-Luc, my Parisian tortured-artist type. He paints me, he paints on me, we paint and pant all over the place. Tommy plays second base for the Chicago Cubs and we collide whenever we're both in New York together. Tommy smells of sunshine and Scotch. He has the best body, but he's not as smart as the others, and so on, and so on. There are more, I'm afraid.

Needless to say, I am true to my "spirited" self in all of these fantasies. My men wouldn't have it any other way. The only hitch is that my lover-in-every-port fantasy runs smack into the wall of my getting-married-to-Luke-the-minute-I-graduate fantasy.

I do my best not to have them at the same time.

"Don't try to distract me with that lusty girl stuff, Sarah Irene Davis. What was IT like?"

We went upstairs to chisel off the masks.

"Well? Well?" I demanded in between splashings.

"Well," said Sarah, towelling off her face. "It's hard to put into words."

"Oh no you don't!" I'd hit the jackpot here. This was the Holy Grail of information. "I need words, Sarah. Find the words!"

She sighed. "Well, you know how they all say that the first time is all awkward and uncomfortable and even painful?"

I didn't know "they" all said that, but some of the romance books alluded to that, so I nodded knowingly.

"Well, it's not, at least for me it wasn't," she giggled. "It was lovely and delicious." She hugged herself.

"Okay," I nodded. "That's good. But what happened exactly? I really don't know as much as you'd think I'd know." Well, that was an understatement. I swear Mama timed all our moves so that I would miss each and every one of the most pertinent sex-ed classes. I sure couldn't ask her about any of this. She had to be medicated when I insisted on using tampons. And I didn't want to get into the technical stuff with the Aunties.

We sat side by side on her bathroom floor. Sarah talked about touches and tongues, and heat and shivers, and fumbling and caressing. I was still completely fuzzy on the mechanics, but I was getting all worked up.

"'*She ignored his teasing, but it was impossible to ignore the demands of his lips and his hands on her bare, sweat-slippery body,*'" I recited.

"What?" said Sarah.

"Page 264, *Sweet Savage Love*. It was just like that, right? And that's just the way it would be with Luke."

She frowned. "Yeah, I guess it was, sort of." Then she sort of disappeared for a minute and then returned. "So, how are you with all of that?"

"Kind of tingly, to tell you the truth."

"No, doorknob," she hit my arm. "With keeping it a secret?"

"Oh, oh that." I nodded. For some reason, I got mad at Madison all over again. "Sure, it's your story, you tell it when you're ready. Just don't sit on it forever, you know?"

Sarah inhaled deeply. "And, um, you don't think I'm, well, that I, because I've given a lot of thought to that part, you don't think I'm *loose,* do you? It's what nature intended after all and naturally natural and so, do you think I'm morally . . ."

She started rearranging sofa cushions.

Oh, right. There was *that.* Whoa, yeah, uh, maybe, probably . . . but this was Sarah. If it weren't Sarah, uh, then yeah, but it was, so? I was going to have to sort all that out—at some point—in the distant future. "Sarah," I said. "I think you're sweet and adorable and I'm honoured that you're my friend."

And that was the truth.

She reached over and hugged me. "I love you, Sophie."

There was a sudden commotion downstairs, doors slamming, dogs barking, kids laughing. The rest of the Davis women were back from Brownies.

"Dinner's ready, girls!" called Mrs. Davis.

"Come on," said Sarah. She yanked me up.

Wait, wait. It hit me that not only was Sarah *not* going to marry this boy, but she didn't even mention anything about wanting to date him. That rattled and roared inside of me so much that I started to get seasick. It was too confusing. So I refused to think about it.

My mind may have been boggling but not enough that it stopped me from incorporating all the new information into my Sophie-the-secret-service-agent fantasy. I went down the stairs slowly, majestically, as befit my new status. I, Sophie Kandinsky, was now in possession of some serious, hard-core, semi-clear information. I was an entirely different person than I had been a mere forty-five minutes ago.

I wondered whether everyone would be able to tell just by looking at me.

Dinner felt like a picnic. Kentucky Fried Chicken is, hands down, the finest food in the universe. Who knew? Not only that, but it comes in these gigantic red-and-white buckets filled with brilliant chicken and even more brilliant French fries. And to top it all off, the whole meal comes with its own implements *and* a full array of condiments! Not that I'd ever been on one, but dinner had that whole silly "isn't this fun and oh so carefree" kind of feel to it that the picnics in the TV commercials do.

Mr. Davis arrived during the unpacking pandemonium and cheerfully loosened his tie as he took his place at the head of the table. "Hiya, Sophie. I see that in honour of your first dinner with this family, my wife has gone all out."

Mrs. Davis threatened him with a drumstick. "Now, Bob, you know that tonight was Brownie night."

"Don't believe a word of it, Sophie." He got up to help himself to the French fries and to a bit of Mrs. Davis. "Every night is some kind of something-or-other-night around here." Then he kissed her.

Right on the lips!

Jesus, the whole family was out of control.

Mama would've knocked Papa flat.

I'm pretty sure Madison's parents never touch and the Cormiers were in the process of getting a divorce so . . .

Mrs. Davis tossed a towelette at him.

No one else seemed to notice just how bizarre this all was.

The girls kept up a constant barrage of teacher complaints, fashion comments, and the latest romance gossip. The entire Davis clan, including the parents, seemed to keep a running tab on who had a crush on whom and how it was all going. Just as Susie came in with what was left of Sarah's lemon poppyseed cake, supplemented by three different tubs of ice cream, Sarah nudged me under the table and then mouthed, "This is a present."

Present?

"Oooo, I have something." Everyone turned to look at Sarah in such well-practised unison that I could only conclude that she must be considered an excellent family source for the latest poop on people. "Methinks, perchance, that there might be trouble brewing with Northern's premier couple, the lovely and oh-so-golden Alison Hoover and Luke Pearson."

Jesus. What was she doing?

"Oh, really?" said Mrs. Davis, like she knew what Sarah was talking about.

"Yup," nodded Sarah, reaching for the chocolate-choco-late-chip ice cream.

"Remind me again, just how long have they been an item?" asked Mrs. Davis.

Wow, this was like talking to the Aunties.

Sarah pretended to search for the answer. "Couple years maybe, almost," she shrugged. "But he's got that itchy look you talk about, Mum."

"Hmmmn," Mrs. Davis hmmned.

"And . . . she's clinging to him like a barnacle."

"Ahhh." The whole table nodded.

"Well, then." Mr. Davis shook his head. "Her days are numbered."

Sarah turned to me and beamed.

"I agree," said Mrs. Davis. "And let that be a lesson to all you Davis girls, you too, Sophie. No clinging. It makes young men claustrophobic. They need the illusion of space. For Luke and Alison, well, it's all over but the shouting. I'm afraid I never liked her mother much anyway. All of the Hoovers have entitlement issues."

I *loved* these people. Maybe they could adopt me. I'd be a real help with the new baby.

When I finally went to leave, the Davises all lined up to give me a hug goodbye. All of them. What an incredibly phys-ical family, especially for Blondes.

I headed home full of chicken and hugs and certain in the knowledge that Luke and Alison were a thing of the past. Maybe it was time to start hinting to Mama about Luke. Yeah, maybe I should. I turned on all the lights as soon as I got in.

Pure habit. When every light in the place is blazing, you don't feel so alone.

Which I wasn't.

Papa was sitting at the kitchen table in the somewhat-dark.

"Papa?"

"Hi, Princess."

"Papa, what were you doing all alone in the dark?"

"Is it dark?" He looked confused.

"Well, no, I just turned on the . . . are you okay?"

And then I saw it. Beside his ashtray. Beside the package of Rothmans, beside him.

A brandy, two fingers of lovely amber liquid in a juice glass.

"How was your dinner with the little dumpling and the dumpling's family?" He meant Sarah.

"Great," I said. "They're all kind of sweet and soft and . . ."

"Dumplingish?"

"Yeah," I nodded. "You'd like them." Where was the brandy bottle? I scanned the kitchen and casually sauntered into the living room. "And you'd love this amazing, brilliant Kentucky Fried Chicken stuff we had for dinner. It was like a picnic and . . ."

Not on the coffee table.

"It really was finger-licking good, just like on the commercials, Papa."

Not by the couch. "Where's Mama?"

I could hear him snort. "The hotshot real estate career woman is, where else, out showing houses."

He took another swig. "Again."

I was calm. Not *pretending* to be calm, but *calm*.

I remembered this. It felt familiar. In a weird way it was comforting. Where was the bottle?

"Sit down, Princess." He patted the kitchen chair beside him. "You don't have to worry."

I sat across from him and leaned over. "I'm not worried, Papa, really."

He shook his head and smiled, his hair falling into his eyes, and for a second, just in that one small gesture, he looked like a little boy. "It's my second brandy, no more, no less. I've never had more than two since getting . . . leaving the . . ."

His eyes were clear, no storms over the ocean, he smelled like Papa, *and* his hands were steady. My God, seven years and all the checkpoints came to me automatically. "I know you don't lie to me, Papa."

"That's right, Princess. That's because we have the real deal."

"Yeah, we do."

I kept scanning the room. I couldn't stop myself. "So, where's the bottle, Papa?"

"I'm writing a poem about you, Princess. I started writing it today. About the miracle that is you and about stolen years found."

"Oh, Papa, for me? That's so . . . wow, for me? You're writing again? Cool."

He downed the brandy in one gulp, got up, rinsed out his glass and left it to dry on the counter. I'd have to wash it out with dishwashing liquid and dry it properly later. "Yes, I'm writing." He kissed the top of my head. "For the first time in many, many years, yet another miracle. It's called 'Sophia Lost and Found.'"

"Really! Can I read it?"

Papa glanced back hungrily to the counter, to the drying empty glass. "Ah, see, there are some things you have forgotten. It will be weeks, maybe months, before I can let you see it. But it's about you and for you and that's all you have to know for now." He kissed me again and then started rattling around for the Turkish coffee utensils.

"Coffee, Princess?"

"Yes, Papa."

"Eva says you like it strong with lots of sugar, right?"

"What's this? All of a sudden you're talking to Auntie Eva? I thought you two hated each other."

"Correction, she hates me." He turned on the stove. "I only hate her because she hates me, but she started it." I could hear him chuckling. "Eva calls looking for Mama, who, as we know, is never here, so she is forced to talk to me."

"Papa, it's only because . . ."

He walked over and kissed the top of my head again. "I know how devoted the old bat is to you *and* to your mother. Believe me, I know."

He poured our coffee. "Oh, and another little miracle. As of today, I have one more part-time temporary job!"

"That's great, Papa! More translating?"

"No, I'm going to be doing the 'What's Up this Week' notices at the *Polska Prawda* until the regular woman comes back from giving birth. It's only two afternoons a week."

"But that's perfect. It leaves you some time to finish my poem."

He cupped my face in his hand.

"Yes, yes it does, Princess."

Papa whistled as he retrieved our tiny coffee cups. Papa doesn't whistle like any ordinary man. He blows out entire movie scores from *The Good, the Bad, and the Ugly* or *An American in Paris.* I could listen to him whistling forever.

I had to find the place.

It wasn't in the cupboard above the fridge. That was an old favourite. I checked last week, empty. But then again, he used to move it around.

I used to know all his places in our other places.

We hardly had any furniture here. Mama turfed most of our second-hand stuff when we moved into the condo. Our "fresh" start was going to include "fresh" furniture, sleek, modern, first-class-only kind of stuff, like the condo, like our new lives. We were saving up.

Papa caught me looking around at our nearly empty dining and living area. "One more surprise, Princess, but this one is a secret."

Of course it is.

"Do you know what I'm doing with Želko?"

Ohhh boy, Želko was Papa's best buddy from before. He was a freelance carpenter/artist. He and Papa made me a full-length mirror for my eighth birthday that is one of the wonders of the world. Madison says that it's absolutely museum quality. Thing is, Želko drinks a bit. I was pretty sure that if Mama knew about any of this, she'd have a fit and not let Papa out to play with Želko any more.

"No, Papa, what?"

"We are making a completely handcrafted dining room table out of this amazing oak."

I thought of my diary.

I thought of Mama's dreams of a sleek and modern dining room.

Jesus God.

"And we're carving whole scenes into each of the legs of flowers and trees from Mama's village in Bulgaria. She'll weep when she sees it."

Yup.

"I'm also going to carve in some swans. She used to love swans. There were these swans we would feed in the lake in High Park when you were little. Remember, Sophia?"

I didn't, but I didn't have the heart to tell him. I nodded.

"It will seat six, so all of your crazy Aunties can come and sit at Mama's fabulous dining room table and we'll laugh and eat and she'll love it and brag to everyone, and then we'll laugh some more."

"And we'll get Kentucky Fried Chicken to put on the table with the goulash!" What can I say, I totally bought it. I always did.

"For sure."

"And, Papa? About the . . ."

"It really was only two brandies."

"I know, Papa."

"It would upset her needlessly, you know how she is."

"Absolutely," I said.

9

I got up at 5:30 A.M. It took an hour and a half to shower, do my hair, and then put on layers and layers of makeup so that it would look like I wasn't wearing any. Luke liked a fresh face. Actually he said that he liked *my fresh face.* He said it last spring, Thursday, May 22, between third and fourth period in the second-floor hallway, to be exact.

So for the first few weeks this year, I just wore clear lip gloss, until it hit me that a "fresh face" was the kind of thing a guy admires about his kid sister. Alison Hoover, Luke's barnacle, wore tons of makeup. So, then I started piling on the eyeliner and foundation, but the Blondes insisted that I looked just this side of Cruella De Vil, which apparently wasn't my best look. I spent the first month of school washing off my makeup in the third-floor washroom (best lighting) by second period and then reapplying it by fourth period. I had the same schizoid routine at Mike's on Saturday mornings. Just like last year, the senior football team always came in after Saturday practice. Luke was still sweet and everything but kind of uncomfortable-looking around me.

And a bit distant.

It made me mental.

But today, this Saturday, would be different. I just felt it. Maybe it was the Davises' unanimous observation that Alison was "toast." Maybe it was all my newfound "womanly knowledge." Whatever it was, I was going to work fully armed with my "not so natural, natural" look and wearing the padded lilac bra that the Aunties had bought me last month for "special." A dash of Bonne Bell's strawberry lip gloss, a splash of Jean Naté, and I was ready for battle.

You would've thought that the rather high melodrama of the past few months, given the resurrection of my "dead" dad and everything, would've thrown me off of the Luke obsession. I'm ashamed to say the obsession was probably worse. I thought about Lucas Pearson non-stop. When he was in my head, he took up a lot of room, pretty much all of it, to tell the truth. I floated around in a daze, fumbling with feelings I didn't know what to do with, feelings that only Rosemary Rogers and maybe Sarah knew about.

All this sadly confirmed what I'd suspected all along. I am a deeply shallow and self-centred young lady, albeit one with a fabulous quasi-natural glow to her at the moment.

Mike didn't notice my glow.

"Hiya, kid. Ready for the onslaught?" And then he started whistling "Lady of Spain."

Mike never whistled, and for good reason: unlike Papa, he sucked. Wonderful man, lousy whistler. When he was all done with "Lady of Spain," he wrestled "Strangers in the Night" to the ground while I filled up the ketchup and mustard bottles.

By the time I got to the salt and pepper shakers, Mike had moved on to something completely unrecognizable and Bob, our perennial bachelor who always got to Mike's early to claim his spot at the counter, had had enough.

"Mike, old man, what's up with the tunes? I've been coming in here for five years and I've never heard you whistle before."

I would've asked too, but I was way too preoccupied with whether I should dash into the ladies' room and apply more blush or wash it all off.

"Love, Bob, love." Mike looked like he was threatening to launch into an aria. "You should try it, it's a beautiful thing, ain't it, Sophie?" He winked at me.

Ain't what? Did he know about Luke? Had he guessed? Did everyone on the planet know about Luke except Luke? I made a mental list of who might know my secret: the Blondes of course. Then Sarah had probably told her whole family, which meant that half the Brownies and Girl Guides in Toronto knew by now. Then there were the Aunties, and, of course, Papa, and finally, Alison, because, well, the girlfriend usually knows these things . . . wait a minute—LOVE—Mike?

Mike and Auntie Luba?

Last year, I had accidentally rekindled an ancient romance between Auntie Luba and my larger-than-life employer when the Aunties took me out for dinner at Mike's after a basketball game. Apparently they were quite the teenage item in Budapest a thousand years ago. As of last year, Mike was freshly divorced and Auntie Luba was fairly freshly widowed (Uncle Boris died eleven years ago). Sparks flew that night and they had been "keeping company" ever since.

Keeping company was one thing, "love" was quite another. Love implied intense feeling-type things, like the feeling-type feelings I had for Luke. But Mike and Auntie Luba had to be almost fifty, *eew*. It was too gross for words. They were too old to do "intensity." I could barely do intensity. Intensity sucked. They must be doing some other kind of thing.

At precisely 11:17, the football team stormed in, your basic Barbarians at the Gate scenario, loud, crude . . . besides, intensity doesn't last, except in *Sweet Savage Love*. In real life, that kind of intensity is called a "phase." Yeah. That's it. Luke was a phase. *Seventeen* magazine had an article about it in the September issue. Like, one minute you're obsessed to the point of stalking the guy and the next, it's over. Jesus, I was probably over Luke and didn't even realize it because I didn't think of it as a possibility, but now that I considered that it might be a possibility, yes, I was certainly over . . .

"Hi, Sophie." Luke flashed me his one-dimple smile.

Or not.

Get a grip. I had to make this stop. I *hated* feeling so much *feeling*. The next hour, like all Saturdays, was complete chaos. The guys were rowdy and silly. Mike fired up eggs and home fries before I even took the orders. The boys loved giving me a hard time. I threatened the entire offensive line with cutlery several times. They were relatively civilized only during the few seconds it took them to inhale their steak and eggs. I was trying to catch my breath by the blenders when Mike called me over to the cash register.

"Tonight's the big night, kid."

"Wow, that's cool." I nodded. "What big night?"

Mike punched the "no sale" key on the register. The drawer sprung forward and he reached around in the back until he extracted a small blue box.

Neither of us breathed.

"Tonight, I am going to ask my little flower for her hand in marriage."

Little flower, Auntie Luba? The woman was 220 if she was a pound.

"Oh my God, Mike."

He opened the box, revealing a spectacularly gaudy ring in the shape of a sunflower made up of a million tiny diamonds. It was the size of a saucer.

"Whaddaya think?"

"She'll love it. I love it," I answered truthfully.

Mike beamed and stared at the ring lovingly.

"Uh, Sophie?"

It was Luke. He was sitting on the very last stool, the one that bachelor Bob had relinquished as soon as the team came in. Luke had brought me his plates and cutlery all neatly stacked up, just like he always did. According to the Aunties, this was the first solid piece of evidence of his unconscious devotion to me.

"What does a guy have to do to get another cup of coffee around here?" He lifted his cup with his incredibly beautiful, tanned, powerful, large yet gentle . . . Jesus, it was just a hand.

Oh, but what a hand.

"Just whistle," I said. "You know how to whistle, don't ya? You put your lips together and blow."

What the hell? Where did that come from? Someone take a gun and shoot me. I was reciting movie dialogue. I was as bad as Mama. I had Mama sickness.

Luke laughed.

Gorgeous teeth.

"Lauren Bacall," he said. "In *To Have and Have Not,* right? I love that film, Sophie."

I am sooo brilliant. Jesus in Heaven, he watches old movies! Somehow I got the coffee into his cup without spazzing all over the place.

Luke brushed my fingers. "You have such nice hands," he said.

Or I think he said. The blood was pumping so furiously in my ears that I was practically deaf. Did he say I had nice hands, or did I tell him *he* had nice hands? No, he was definitely smiling at *my* hands.

It must be the bra. We'd bought this latest version last month. The Aunties were always on a quest for *the* perfect padded bra for me. My first padded bra had an unfortunate tendency to cave in when I brushed against anything, like a gust of wind, say. This one didn't do that. It had serious underwires and it was so super-stiff that it didn't dent. Its only drawback was that it was too big in the back, so I had to be careful how I moved around or else the whole thing would ride up and the wires would press in the middle of my boobs giving me that oh-so-attractive four-breast look. So far, I had refused to do any reaching for soda glasses or malt vinegar bottles and I still had two good ones.

Apparently we were still talking about old movies and apparently I was participating even though Luke brushed my fingers with the back of his fingers.

That was no accident.

I had an immediate vision, clear as day: Luke rises to his full six-foot-two-inch glory and with a stroke of his powerful wide-receiver arm, he sweeps all the glassware and dishes off the counter. Then he growls sort of, grabs me, and, and does a page 237.

"She knew her struggles were useless . . . he'd take whatever he wanted from her . . . especially when he began to move his hands teasingly and very slowly over her body . . . she felt his lips follow his hands and cried out wildly . . ."

Of course, we are alone in the restaurant while all this ravaging is going on. I love that word. *Ravage.* Now there's a word you can sink your teeth into.

So there I am pretending to struggle on the counter while Luke ravages me over and over again. Finally, spent and cold with fury, Luke says that he hates me, hates how I made him do that and be unfaithful to the barnacle.

I toss my luxurious inky black curls and spit *spiritedly* that "I hate it, too."

"What do you hate?" Luke looked completely puzzled.

Ooops.

Mike launched into a rendition of "Unforgettable."

"I, uh, hate the weirdness of old people," I said. "I mean just look at Mike, it's like he's our age, you know? And that's just wrong."

Luke nodded, but he was being polite. He didn't have a clue what I was talking about. I was barely on board myself.

"Just look," I whispered. Mike was snapping his fingers and doing a little dance step as he cashed out the team.

"He is going to propose to my Auntie Luba tonight and I can tell he's all . . . and she probably will be too, and, like, they must be fifty, you know?"

"I do know." Luke shook his head. "Two years ago, my grandfather divorced my grandmother and then, out of the blue, last June he married his old neighbour. They were, well, you know, for months."

"No guff, your grandfather!"

"Yeah, and I had to be his best man." Luke took a last swig of his coffee. Pete Gallagher, the quarterback, was waiting for him by the cash. "Yeah," he nodded. "It messes with your mind." He probably said other things too but I was watching his mouth so intently that I was transported to the much reread page 133 of my *Sweet Savage Love* playbook when Steve says to Ginny, *'Better go back to your wagon, Miss Brandon,' he said suddenly, harshly, breaking the spell that seemed to have seized them both for an instant. 'Because if you don't I'm liable to grab a hold of you and kiss you—and they're all watching.'*

Whatever Luke was saying, he meant to be saying that grabbing and holding and kissing you stuff. I was sure of it. Then he licked his lips, smiled, and knocked on the counter.

"Later," he said. Really. I mean he *really* did say that.

"Later," I said.

How much later?

I started wiping off the counter.

WHAT is the matter with me? Luke barely touches me and I instantly proceed to a restaurant ravaging? And I had all these pictures in my head. Not enough, mind you, having only Sarah's lusty, but still vague, description and ditto Rosemary Rogers's. I knew I was still missing a few key details.

I am so bad.

I might as well get tattooed and drop some acid.

My skin felt too tight.

And I was pulsing.

10

The Aunties were on fire. An all-points bulletin was sent out for an immediate, emergency summit. We were marshalled into Auntie Eva's latest triplex for high-level tactical strategizing. The Aunties were levitating. This was big. This was huge. There was a wedding to be planned.

A full three or four minutes were devoted to considering a chaste and decorous little reception reflective of their circumstances, that is, that Mike was, after all, divorced and Auntie Luba was, in fact, a widow. Then there was their age. Mike was forty-nine and Auntie Luba was, well, her age was a more closely guarded secret than the location of NORAD missile silos, but for sure, the bride was no longer blushing. Finally, there was the potential awkwardness of the ethnic diversity thing. Mike was a Macedonian, not a Greek, as Auntie Eva kept insisting, and Auntie Luba was Czechoslovakian.

Given those formidable constraints, we, of course, decided to have a party to end all parties.

Auntie Eva had laid out platters of smoked meats, green onions, and pickled peppers to nourish our creative juices. I put in my two cents on the decorum front by outlining what Madison had described as the likely scenario for a full-on Chandler wedding.

"So, there's, like, maybe seventy-five guests all in the Chandler backyard. Madison, wearing her grandmother's gown, altered to fit of course, would be piped in by a Scottish piper in full regalia. Then Madison would proceed down a garlanded aisle to a canopy made out of beautiful white roses near their pond. Everything is white on white. Naturally, me, Kit, and Sarah will be the bridesmaids."

"But who vill be za best maid?" asked Auntie Eva.

"You mean, maid of honour?"

"Zat is vat I said," said Auntie Eva.

"Ov course, it vill be Sophie," snorted Auntie Luba. "Sophie is za very best friend."

Was I? Was I ever? "Well, don't forget that Kit and Sarah and Madison have known each other for years . . ."

"Phhhft," they all said, even Mama.

Auntie Radmila patted my knee. "Za two of you have come trew fire togezer. Has she told za ozers about za grand-mama?"

I shook my head.

"Madison is a good girl, and she loves our girl. Wherever dey go dey vill go trew it together."

That was Mama. It sounded like she was going to break into song. Mama's drug of choice was old movie musicals and when she got really excited, or especially happy, her English would be peppered with film and song snatches. I hadn't heard her do it in so long that I thought she had grown out of it.

"So good, our little Sophia vill be za best maid at za cheapskate vedding." Auntie Eva seemed comforted by this.

"It is *not* cheap!" I said. "It's very, extremely elegant." I made an immediate note to myself to start competing for the position of maid of honour from that day forward.

"Please," snorted Auntie Radmila. "Zese people are multi-millionaires and zey can't afford a hall? And only seventy-five people! AND don't even getting me to start on za second-hand vedding dress! How many meat courses?"

"No, see, the thing is, it's not like that." I didn't know why I was arguing for this, it sounded pretty dismal even when Madison was dreamily explaining the whole "Chandler Tradition" at the time. "Then, after the ceremony, every-one returns to the house for champagne and exquisite hors d'oeuvres and tea sandwiches."

"No soup even?" asked Auntie Radmila, distaste dripping off of every word.

Auntie Eva shook her head. "Cheap, cheap, cheap."

"But there are all these white roses and garlands and champagne and . . ."

"I really, for sure, like za Scotch man vit za pipes idea. It's a music for a very grand big entrance," said Auntie Luba.

"Please, Luba darling," snorted Auntie Eva. "You're a Slovak, he's a Greek . . ."

"Macedonian," I said.

"Zat is vat I said."

"I love da sound of da pipes," Mama smiled. "Dey are so romantic and so haunting, remember *Brigadoon* vit Gene Kelly and Cyd Charisse, 1954?"

Everyone paused to remember.

"I agree," said Auntie Eva. "Ve vill find a big Scotch man vit a skirt and a pipe."

"Ya." They all nodded.

The piper was in.

Auntie Eva may have been the lead Auntie, but they worshipped Mama. If Mama thought pipes were romantic, pipes it was. Auntie Eva bounded off to search for paper and a pen. "And seventy-five peoples! Zat wouldn't even cover Luba's peoples. And zat Mike, he is a big man in his community. Zose Greeks like a big party."

"Macedonians," I said.

"Zat is vat I said."

I swear, I couldn't stop myself. "No, you *said* Greek." Maybe it was her disparaging remarks about Madison's wedding.

"Phhhft!" She lit a cigarette and shrugged. "Iz za same ting."

I gave up.

"Well, Auntie Luba, what do you want for your wedding? You told me that you and Uncle Boris couldn't afford any kind of reception when you got married."

Auntie Luba cupped my face with both of her hands. "Sophia, little buboola, I vant a big, big party to celebrate my brand new big, big life vit Mikos."

"Ya!" Everyone but Mama and me raised their brandy glass and downed it. We downed our orange juice. If Mama weren't there, I'd be swigging brandy with the Aunties.

Mama put her arm around Auntie Luba. "Ve vill make you party to finish all parties, Luba. Four lambs and three pigs on a spit, schnitzel, soup, a band, flowers absolutely everyplace and not just vite vons. I vill do everybody's makeup, ve vill get Mrs. McClintock to do all da dresses, and you vill be a qveen, I promise, Luba, a qveen."

Auntie Luba beamed and teared up at the same time.

Wow, I'd almost forgot just how good Mama could be.

"Ya, a qveen already." Auntie Eva went for the brandy bottle. "So! Ve need Greek musicians, Slovak musicians, and a JD for Sophia's friends."

"DJ," I corrected, but my heart wasn't in it. My friends? My friends were being invited to this spectacle?

"And," Auntie Eva refilled glasses, "maybe you vill invite za beautiful boy who you vill hit vit a ton of bricks ven he sees you in your dropping dead flower girl outfit."

"Flower girl?!"

"Vat beautiful boy?" asked Mama softly.

"Oh, it's nothing, Mama." My face got hot. I felt guilty. But why should I feel guilty? She was the one who was never around. When was I supposed to tell her? "Luke Pearson, I've got a crush on him, but he's been going steady with Alison Hoover for two years so there's no chance . . ."

"Phooey," sniffed Auntie Eva. "Even your Papa tinks he's crazy for you."

"Papa has met him?" Mama whispered.

"Yeah," I shrugged. Something was wrong, but I couldn't put my finger on it. "By accident, remember when he took the Blondes and me to Fran's that once?"

"A boy," Mama nodded. She didn't look angry. I thought she would be angry, but she didn't look angry. It was confusing.

"Hey!" I tapped on the table. "What do you mean flower girl?" We had to get back to the controversy at hand. "There is no such thing as a fifteen-year-old flower girl! I can't be a flower girl."

Auntie Luba looked devastated. "But I alvays vanted a flower girl, and it vouldn't be right for Eva or Radmila, now vould it?"

She had me there.

"Your Mama is za best maid and Radmila and Luba vill be my bridesmaids. Perfect, no?"

"Okay, okay." What can I say? I got all caught up in the harmony of the moment and agreed that it was all better than perfect. "So when's the happy day?"

"December 13. Ve booked za Hungarian Hall already. It's not so busy in December."

"Zat's because only crazy people get married in December." Auntie Eva raised her glass in a toast.

They clinked their glasses. "To crazy people!"

"Wow," I said. "You guys have only been dating for a few months and now you're getting married in a couple of months?"

"Ya," Auntie Luba sighed. "It has been a real virling in za vind romance and now ve vill have a real virling vind vedding. Zat's za best kind, eh, Magda."

Mama blushed. Mama and Papa met, fell in love, and got married all in the space of a month. When I was little, and through all the prison years, I would ask her to break it down for me, day by day, hour by hour, and then I would correct her if she got one of the bits wrong. It was one of our favourite games.

The rest of the evening whizzed by in the high drama of potential fabric and flower choices. Auntie Radmila was appointed Auntie Eva's official escort to the fabric stores for the first pass on dress materials. This only happened because it was an open secret that Auntie Eva was colour blind, which has led to some entertaining choices in the past. She usually won't buy a thing unless Mama checks it over.

We decided on the full treatment, absolutely formal floor-length gowns and tuxedos. But Auntie Luba would not be wearing white. White was simply too simple, not nearly "big" enough. I suspected that ostrich feathers and sequins would be heavily featured.

Mama would do the flowers. A job any of the Aunties would have killed for. I always marvelled over how much power Mama held in that little group. She was so much younger and they adored her and yet . . . I couldn't prove this, but I'd bet my box of romance novels that they were a little afraid of her. For all their largeness, loudness, and thunderous personalities, Mama was tougher.

Despite this, Auntie Eva somehow convinced her to let me have "just von brandy, just this vonce, for za celebration." Mama surprised us all by agreeing. I was so stunned that I forgot to act surprised by the bite of the brandy. We toasted the future bride. We toasted the future groom. We toasted the best maid and we toasted the bridesmaids. When it came to toasting me, the flower girl, Mama got up and raised her glass.

My breath snagged on a hook. Mama's hands. There wasn't a vainer woman on the planet about her hands than my Mama. Her nail polish was chipped and ratty looking, her nails broken and uneven.

"To Sophie, who has become a voman ven I just looked avay for a moment."

But she smiled when she said it.

Lately, my place had become *the* preferred place. For one thing, Madison, Kit, and Sarah genuinely got a kick out of Papa, and for another, since Papa smokes like a chimney, the condo always reeked, so they had a much easier time sneaking a cigarette.

This latest meeting had been called to discuss plans for our appearance at Auntie Luba and Mike's wedding. The Blondes never went to any party without a party plan fully developed well ahead of the event. The plan would cover behaviour, potential conquests, outfits, makeup, and backup contingencies. Madison always kept in her mind, and therefore ours, our "position" and "image" in the school and every outing had to either solidify or enhance our overall standing.

Apparently, maintaining popularity took as much strategizing as the invasion of Normandy, but here I was right in the eye of the personal popularity hurricane. Given that until the Blondes, I had only experienced the hurricane part at the other schools, I was still stunned by it all. At least the shallow, self-centred part of me was.

And that, let's face it, was a pretty big part.

Madison rooted around my cupboards looking for all the Turkish coffee paraphernalia. Papa had got the Blondes hooked on the stuff by November. Madison always got the coffee for us. It was her version of a highly efficient nurture impulse. "Okay, ladies," she called from the kitchen. "Escort potentials?"

"How about Jake Westerhall for you? He's been following you around the school like a lost puppy and he's a senior," said Kit.

It was Madison's contention that, even though we were only in grade ten, we were poised to rule by next year, so we had to be extra careful about our public appearances this year. She put the carafe to boil and then joined us. "But he's not even on the football team."

Kit shook her head. "Madison, Madison. This is why I am indispensable to this group as a whole, and to you in particular, my dear. Jake is not on the football team because he plays Junior B hockey. Junior B trumps high school football on any measurable status scale."

Madison weighed this carefully and turned to Sarah. "Sarah, you really do need a suitably impressive escort. Make Rodney Meyers adore you."

Sarah shrugged listlessly.

"Kit," she said. "I assume Rick is still yours for the asking?"

"Oh, I can bring him around again," said Kit. "But I don't know, I think I broke up with him the last time because I really wanted to break up with him. The magic has pretty well petered out."

"But he's a star running back this year!" Madison was handing out the little coffee cups.

Kit shrugged.

"This is pathetic," groaned Sarah.

"Whoa, lambchop!" Kit coughed on her coffee. "Have we slipped into some parallel universe? You love this crap."

"Well, what do we even need guys for?" She groaned again.

Our jaws dropped. If nothing else, Sarah was so not a groaner.

"No, look, I mean it's a Sophie/Auntie love fest, all ethnic music, bear hugs, and tons of food, right?"

Whoa. Was I being trashed? By Sarah?

"You're absolutely right, sweetcheeks!" Kit slapped her on the back. "We'll be in the Sophie bubble. Lots of crazy music, crazy dancing, crazy food . . ."

I may have overdone the Eastern European aspect of all this.

"So . . .," Sarah nodded. "How about we go with just us, no game plan, no image dates, just us, friends having fun. What a concept, eh?"

"Well . . .," sniffed Madison.

"Come on, Madison, lighten up." Kit was the only one of us who could get away with that. "Who's going to know? Let's just go and have ourselves a hoot!"

Madison groaned prettily. Madison *was* a groaner but she did it fetchingly. You had to hand it to her. I've tried that in front of the mirror, over and over again. It's right up there with crying fetchingly, which she also does. "Okay, what the hell, count me in," she said. "Let's just celebrate Mike and Luba's big juicy wedding, with just us."

I loved her all over again.

"That's my fearless leader." Kit patted her on the head. "So, Soph, do we roast the pigs on the spit ourselves or what?"

I had definitely overdone it. "No, I told you that's done by the Croatian caterers, but here's the latest itinerary, pay attention:

Live band, so non-stop dancing.
Open bar.
Ten-course meal at 7:00 which really means 9:30, so eat a bit before you come or else you'll get too loaded.
Dessert at 11:30.
Midnight buffet at 2:00 A.M.
The bride and groom leave around 4:00 A.M. after the bouquet toss.

And that, ladies, in a nutshell, is the reception and, oh yeah, keep in mind that there will be about four hundred guests."

"Yeah baby!" said Kit. "That just sounds *so* much better than my cousin's crappy reception at the club."

"You can say that again," said Madison. "I may have to incorporate a couple of these details into the Chandler Tradition."

"I can't wait to try the pig on a spit thing," said Sarah. "It's going to be the best bash ever."

I loved my Blondes.

Kit looked at her watch. "Damn, girls, it's nine o'clock. I promised my dad I'd be back by nine. He needs the car tonight."

"But we haven't finished all the Turkish coffee yet," said Madison.

"Sophie and I will drink it," said Sarah. "We have some chem homework we have to do."

It was news to me.

"But the . . ."

Kit yanked Madison up. "Sophie promises to let you make another cup real soon. Let's go or I'm busted."

"What chemistry homework?" I asked when the elevator doors shut. Sarah shrugged.

She started pacing as soon as we got back to the condo.

"Sarah, what's up?"

She shrugged again and then groaned.

"Sarah, you're starting to freak me out. Sarah . . ."

"I'm in trouble, Sophie. Or, I could be, but I might not be. In fact, probably not, but I don't know how to know, you know?"

"Uh . . . no."

"It's a secret."

Of course.

"Okay, a secret," I agreed.

"*They* can't know."

"Who, Madison and Kit?"

"Swear."

"I swear already, what? What!?"

"I may be in trouble, but maybe not, but I don't know."

"SARAH! We did that part already."

"I, it could be . . . that I may be, it's possible that . . . I might be . . ."

"Sarah!"

"Pregnant."

The word landed on the floor with a thud. We both looked down. Neither of us breathed until the refrigerator motor kicked in and startled me into action.

"Uh . . .," I said.

"Yeah," she said.

We fell into the couch. "The counsellor guy?"

She nodded.

"He's, like, in university right?"

She nodded.

"Okay, so that's, like, statutory rape or something."

"Oh, that's helpful, Sophie." She grabbed a pillow and hugged it tight. "Besides . . . I practically raped him."

This was surreal. "Jesus." There's no way we were having the conversation that we were having. I got up to get the rest of the coffee. I did this in a state of slow motion, semi-delirium. I, Sophie Kandinsky, was the friend of a friend who maybe was . . .

"Okay, so fine. He'll have to marry you. We'll have a double wedding, Mike and Auntie Luba and you and . . . what's his name again?"

"Andrew."

I decided to hate that name. "A double wedding with you and Andrew. Are you still seeing him?"

"I told you, I broke up with him at the end of camp. It was only a summer fling."

"Sarah . . ."

"Okay, maybe I *saw* him a couple more times after that, but I broke it off for good by the end of October and that's the truth, honest. I knew it was wrong, or fairly wrong because . . . I don't love him, Sophie, I just sort of talked myself into it at the time, each time, because you're supposed to . . . and I didn't . . . thing is, I just really wanted to . . ."

And then, I seemed to lose her.

"Sarah!" I snapped my fingers in her face. "Okay, no wedding. We'll look into a home for unwed mothers. It's a big city. Toronto must be bursting with that kind of thing, or maybe a place in the country, with nice fields and a pond . . ."

A look of abject terror crept onto her face and moved in.

"Or a really glamorous spa-like place in Beverly Hills. Your folks are loaded. Yeah, you go away and then come back with really nice skin and your mother comes back with a baby and raises it as her own! It's done all the time in Hungarian villages. Auntie Eva is full of those stories, minus the Beverly Hills part, of course." She was looking at me like I had two heads.

"Right, your mom is already pregnant." I combed my brain for the right phrase. "Uh, how far are you gone?"

"See, that's just it. I don't know that I am."

"Am what?"

"Gone. I'm not at all sure I'm *gone*."

We sipped our coffee.

"Well then, we have to find out."

"Exactly."

"Exactly."

"How, Sophie?"

I did more memory combing and scrolled through all of the "inappropriate" conversations with the Aunties around the topic of sex and babies. "So, you've missed your period?"

She leaned back into the sofa. "Yeah, I think, maybe."

I didn't jump all over her for that one. I mean who really pays attention? It happens when it happens.

"I should've started a couple of weeks ago, I think." She bit her lip. "But thing is, I've missed it big time in the past, even when I was a virgin."

Was a virgin. WAS.

Jesus, God.

What *could* it be like to think of yourself as "was a virgin"? I tried it on for size.

Scary.

"I mean, I've gone weeks and just before I turned fifteen, I missed it for months, so . . ."

"Yeah, and then there's someone like me who didn't even start until I was almost fifteen and as a result, still don't have any breasts to speak of and . . ."

"Sophie!" She snapped her fingers in my face. "Can we stick to *my* crisis? I mean I love you dearly, but you do tend to go off on tangents."

"Sorry, sorry. You're right, we have to find out for sure. That's all that matters. Hey, how about your family doctor?"

All the Blondes had family doctors. We didn't have doctors.
If Mama or I got crazy sick with something we went to the
nearest emergency department.

"No chance." Sarah shuddered. "Dr. Lively delivered me.
He comes to our house for dinner."

Eew. How creepy was that? But then again, it might be better
than having dinner with the ex-cons and semi-sober poets that
Papa snuck home on the nights Mama was showing houses.

"Okay, not your doctor, another anonymous-type doctor
that we find in the phone book. We pretend you're married,
we get a ring, your husband is in the service, yeah, but he's
stationed in, in . . ." There wasn't a single decent war that
Canadians were in, we were a pathetically peace-loving
nation. My country had let me down. "In the North Pole and
I'm your sister . . ."

Sarah got up and grabbed my arms. "Stop, stop, stop."
Apparently, I was the one who was pacing now. "First of all,
there is no way in hell anyone is going to take us for sisters."

Okay, so, she had at least four inches and several cup sizes
on me. That, and Sarah was the blondest of the Blondes. I, on
the other hand, get mistaken for Persian on a fairly regular
basis. Maybe she had a point.

"So?" she said. We had stopped pacing in the kitchen.
Sarah slid down against the cupboards until she reached the
floor. I slid down beside her.

"So, the Aunties would know about stuff like this."

"No. They know me, Sophie, I couldn't stand that they
know."

"I could bring it up anonymously."

"Not a chance," she said. "I've seen them work you over. They'd have it out of you in five minutes."

I didn't bother denying it.

"Buffalo," I said.

"Buffalo?"

"Yeah, Buffalo, New York. It's always bandied about in situations like this. We'd get on the bus, believe me, I know from buses."

"Sophie! Buffalo only comes up when it comes to football and backroom abortions."

"Jesus, you're right. We don't even know if we have a Buffalo-type situation here or not. And if we did have a Buffalo situation, well, I got to warn you that I'm vaguely Catholic on Papa's side and, well, I suppose I could . . ."

"Sophie, tangent alert! Can we cross that bridge when we come to it?"

"Sorry." I put my arm around her. "Look, you're barely two weeks late. I will find out how to find out. I promise. I'm good at finding things out."

I winced. Jesus, the last time I made that promise I ended up tracking down Edna for Madison, which just opened up such a can of secret worms. And things haven't been the same with us since, not really.

"Sophie?"

"This isn't just a secret, but if it comes right down to it, you have to lie your face off. Right?"

I definitely had to revise my diary goals. The "no more" lies thing was completely shot.

"Can you do that, Sophie?"

"Sarah." I turned to her. "You *do* remember that my father was in prison and you all thought he was dead, right?"

"Right, sorry, I don't know how I forgot about that."

I got up slowly and then pulled her up. "Don't worry. I'm on it. I'll figure out something soon, I promise."

She hugged me, hard.

"I knew I picked right."

A not-so-little part of me reared up. What is it about me that makes me the go-to girl for all this kind of stuff? Hell, *was* I only "in" because I knew where all the bodies were buried? I would've gone down that road for a good long self-obsessive stroll, but Sarah started shaking.

I'm proud to say that everything changed on a dime. I put my arms around her and stopped being all confused and scared for myself.

And I started being all confused and scared for her.

I had it as soon as I woke up the next morning. The library! I don't know why I didn't think of it immediately. Librarians are the world's best-kept secret. They know everything worth knowing and, if they don't know, they know exactly where to look so that they will know. Okay, not all of them. Some librarians hate people in general, and hyperactive, motor-mouth girls in specific. Most of them are pretty good though and at least one is beyond brilliant, Mrs. Theodora Setterington, the Answer Lady at the Toronto Central Library.

Mrs. Setterington would know where to go to find out if you were "in trouble." More important, she'd tell me. Mrs. Setterington knows more than everything. I found this out all those years ago when Papa was first charged with manslaughter. By the time the trial actually started, the library was my second home. Between going to school for her real estate licence, selling Mary Kay in Anglican ladies' living rooms, *and* having to be in court, Mama was never home. So, I was either with one of the Aunties, or at the library with Mrs. Setterington. She made me feel indispensable.

I knew all the librarians and the assistant librarians personally. Tuesdays and Thursdays were Storytime from 3:30 to 4:30 and Wednesdays were Get to Know Your Library days. I was convinced that I played an important role in the success of these events. I had a particular gift with the seniors, or so Mrs. Setterington always said. Sometimes she let me re-stack the magazines. I *loved* doing that. She would put on her half-moon glasses and inspect my handiwork very thoroughly.

"Well, my . . .," she'd say in her chocolatey voice, "I simply don't know what we'd do here without you, Sophia."

You'd think I was contributing to "peace in our time."

What a pest I must have been.

I went back to the Central Library no matter where we were living. I went and I told the whole truth to Mrs. Setterington, no matter what the truth was. All through all those horrible times, years and years, I went. And then, when we moved here, and I finally had friends and Papa was home and things were about as good as it gets—I hadn't been once.

Well, I couldn't stop and think about what that said about me. I'd think about that later.

Right now, I needed information.

I went straight after Mike's.

I was so preoccupied by my information-gathering quest that I barely flirted with Luke.

Barely, but I did.

I couldn't stop and think about what that said about me either.

As soon as I stepped through the doors, I could taste the books. I was home.

Mama never let me go to the courtroom. It was her belief that, if I went, it would give me "a mental disease dat would scratch me for life." Little did she know that nothing in the courtroom could match the "mental disease" I was busy giving myself. The trial in my head, cobbled together from black and white repeats of the Perry Mason show, and old "killer on trial" movies, had to be way freakier than what was going on at the courthouse. But then again, when she made me go to visit Papa at the Kingston Penitentiary, I couldn't handle that little taste of reality, so . . .

Basically, Mrs. Theodora Setterington was dealing with an eight-year-old head case when she first came up to me to ask why I was chewing on the pages of library books. Mama and I hadn't yet become the accomplished liars we aspired to be and I blurted out the whole sorry mess in Fiction from M to P. From that day forward, Mrs. Setterington became my ally. She clipped anything at all about Papa's trial that appeared in any of the Toronto papers. She got out legal books and briefs on interlibrary loan and tried to explain in little kid English what it all meant. The only thing that became crystal clear to both of us was that Papa's legal aid lawyer was, as she put it, "a barking idiot." Papa was convicted of manslaughter a year and a half after the murder.

Mrs. Setterington was there through that whole mess and all the messes that came after. There wasn't a single piece of me that wasn't doing cartwheels as soon as I stepped into the library.

I went straight to Reference. Every table had people, books, and papers sprawled all over it, just like always. Quiet chaos. I searched the Reference Desk for Mrs. Setterington and spotted her immediately. A greying cloud of hair that was just a bit whiter and foamier than before. Had she always been so tiny? It looked like the only thing that was keeping her from floating away was her massive profusion of love beads, crystals, and peace symbol jewellery.

I lurked and looked for a long time before I finally walked over to the desk.

She started smiling as soon as she saw me.

"Sophia! Sophia Kandinsky! Hey, babe, how cool is this? Well, look at you, gorgeous! How are you?" She beetled around the desk to give me a hug.

"Great. Unbelievable, so unbelievable you wouldn't believe it, it's that unbelievable."

"Same old Sophia," she chuckled. "Of course I would. I haven't stopped following your father's case. I know all about it, babe. I also know it was the family of a *friend* of yours who started the whole appeal process rolling." Only Mrs. Setterington would know that it was a toss up in miracle lottery as to which was more miraculous: Papa getting out, or me having a friend.

"Yeah, the Chandlers, eh? Madison's my best friend." Did I wince?

Mrs. Setterington put her arm around me and we walked over to History together like we'd just done it yesterday. It was still the most private part of the library.

"And your father?"

"He's great," I said. "He's looking really hard for a full-time job and he's starting to write and he goes to all my games and, and I love him to pieces."

Well, the last bits were a hundred percent true.

And the rest could have been.

I filled her in point form on Northern Heights, Luke, and the basketball team, and, of course, on the Blondes. Okay, I left out the adoption, the puking, and the potentially pregnant parts, for now. One shouldn't overwhelm one's librarian on the first visit.

"Well, of course they like you," she said, settling her slight self on one of those dinky little library footstools. "You're a groovy kid, Sophia."

I retrieved my own footstool and sat down opposite her, resting my back against the Napoleonic Wars. "Oh, and it's Sophie now. Doesn't that sound perfect?"

She smiled at me and didn't say anything for a while. It was like she was trying it on for size. "Hmmmn, Sophie," she nodded. "Yup, pretty perfect."

We sat there for a few minutes, just smiling at each other. Had I ever noticed how beautiful she was before? She had such soft brown eyes and a creamy caramel skin traced by lacy lines that danced around her face every time her expression changed. "You weren't ever a Blonde, were you?"

"No, babe," she chuckled. I am such a sucker for someone who chuckles. "I had gorgeous black hair, just like you."

Gorgeous?

Well, maybe on her.

"So what have you been reading?"

I cringed. Mrs. Setterington had introduced me to Hemingway and Victor Hugo's *Les Misérables*. She talked me through *Crime and Punishment* chapter by chapter. How could I tell her that I was on my fifth read through *Sweet Savage Love*?

"Sophie, if you were capable of blushing, you'd be blushing. What's up? No time for books in your shiny new life?"

I'd never lied to Mrs. Setterington. "No, no, I'm reading all right, it's just . . .," I examined the threadbare carpet between us. "I keep rereading it as a matter of fact."

Her face lit up as my heart sank.

"No, see, it's not like Salinger or anybody, and not only do I keep rereading it and underlining, I even make notes, but I can't seem to stop and . . ."

"Sophie," she interrupted. "What is this miraculous book?"

I looked up. I should make eye contact. I focused on her dreamcatcher earring.

"*Sweet Savage Love* by Rosemary Rogers," I whispered.

She snorted.

And then she began to laugh. You could tell she was trying to "shhh" herself, she was a librarian after all. "Oh, my dear, my Sophie!" Snort, snort. "There's nothing wrong with taking a detour into romance land or whodunit land or whatever land. In fact . . .," she checked the aisle again. "I'm like you, there are times in my life that I simply must retreat into romance. It just helps me get through things."

"You?"

"Yes, me. My default romance book is *The Magnificent Courtesan* by Lozania Prole."

"Oooo, I think I've got that one."

She raised an eyebrow.

"The Aunties came by with a huge romance care-package."

"Ah . . . your Aunties." Mrs. Setterington nodded thoughtfully. "So, babe, I know your life is pretty perfect right now, and you've got Rosemary Rogers for support, but . . ."

I went back to examining the carpet.

"But, well, is there anything you want to talk about, Papa, your friends maybe?"

Right, my friends, my friend. "Well, there is this one *potential* sort of thing."

She nodded and rearranged herself on the footstool.

"Anyway, the thing about Blondes, at least *my* Blondes and, I don't know, probably Blondes generally or worldwide, well, see, some of them are a whole lot more complicated than they look."

"Is that so?"

"No guff. Here you'd think they've got everything— power, popularity, and the hair of course—and all that's true, but there's more to them than just that."

"My," she said.

"Yeah," I gulped, "well, one of them, actually the least complicated one when you come to think of it, has the most complicated situation at the moment, and we don't know what to do."

"Sophie . . .," she whispered.

"I swear, I promise, it's not me."

She reached across and put her hands on my arms.

"Honest, I've never lied to you. It's not me."

"Are we talking about what I think we're talking about?"

Boy, I hoped so. "Probably."

She glanced around, put her finger to her lips until a middle-aged guy finished rummaging through the Crimean War section. "Then you'd better tell me."

"Uh, we don't know how complicated the situation is exactly. We, *she* needs to find out where to go to find out if there is . . . uh . . . if . . . she is . . ."

"She needs to know if she's pregnant." It wasn't a question.

My stomach contracted. "Yes, ma'am, it sounds a lot more serious when you put it that way."

"First of all, don't you start *ma'aming* me at this stage of our relationship, and second, this is *very* serious."

"I know," I mumbled. "But see, maybe not quite as serious as we think. She's done this kind of thing before, missed her period, I mean, sometimes she goes for months without . . ."

Mrs. Setterington stood up. "Stay here."

I stayed glued to the stool, promising myself over and over about how I was going to stay a virgin until my wedding night, maybe even then. Pregnant. It sounded so . . . harsh. I sat there feeling like I was used goods. I couldn't take the guilt, the shame, the tension. Jesus, this was nuts, it wasn't even me.

Then I remembered Luke.

Luke's touch on the small of my back.

Maybe when Luke and I got engaged. I remembered Sarah's hot and dreamy expression as I hounded her for details. Maybe when he gave me his class ring?

"Sophie? Sophie."

Mrs. Setterington crouched down beside me.

"I know you're freaked about your friend. If she is pregnant . . ."

That word again.

"*If* she is pregnant, there are a lot of hard decisions to make. Telling the parents, seclusion, adoption, keeping it, terminating . . ."

Jesus, God. It was like being slapped.

To hell with Luke, I was staying a virgin forever.

Adoption? The whole Madison thing, raising a baby at fifteen? Abortion? Where would you even? Ohmygod, ohmygod.

"Sophie, breathe, honey. First things first, okay?"

I think I nodded.

She handed me a folded piece of paper. "Give her this. They're good people and they'll help no matter what the results are."

I opened the note.

Planned Parenthood

630 College Street

555-2655

"Tell her to ask for Marianne."

I nodded and like so many times over so many years, I reached over and hugged her hard, and like so many times over all those years, Mrs. Theodora Setterington hugged back harder.

"I want you to promise me something," she said.

"Anything."

"When the times comes . . . when you think you're ready for sex, well, keep that address and don't do anything until you've talked to Marianne. I don't care what you think you know, or what your friends have told you, or what you think you know from grade nine health class."

"You don't have to worry about me, Mrs. Setterington. Nobody's touching me until I'm forty."

"Yes, well, be that as it may, arm yourself with information. I mean it, Sophie. Do it for me."

I nodded vigorously. "I promise."

It was a completely unnecessary promise. I had seen the light and it was blinding. There was no way in the world that I was going to have sex with anybody, including Luke Pearson, until there was a ring on my finger.

"You don't have to worry about me," I said, right before leaving.

"No sir," I said to the stacks on the way out. It didn't matter if I was going to be the oldest living virgin in Toronto. I was never putting myself in that kind of predicament, ever. I, Sophie Kandinsky, was never going to star in that kind of movie.

"Not a chance," I said to the street. And I meant it.

We were a five-alarm fire waiting to happen. Auntie Eva's elaborately carved dining room table was a Mount Vesuvius of Butterick, Simplicity, Vogue, and McCall's formal wear patterns. The thin, patterned tissues were cascading every which way, and those that weren't were pinned together in an unholy alliance of Butterick torso, McCall's skirt, and Simplicity arms.

At a minimum, it looked as if our gowns were going to be cobbled together from sixteen different patterns. "Darrrling, zis is how it iz done by anybody who is anybody," Auntie Eva insisted. And Auntie Eva's fashion word was law. She even trumped Mama on this one, colour blind or not. In one of her previous lives, Auntie Eva had actually worn "couture," the real deal. Never mind that it was for one brief season in Paris during her second marriage and that that marriage was annulled, so we didn't really know how to count it. The point was that Auntie

Eva had actually been fitted in a real live Parisian couture house by designer-type people with pins in their mouth. She still possessed an original Dior cocktail dress that had pride of place in her walk-in closet. Sure the size was a distant memory, but we all admired it fiercely and often. So, when Auntie Eva swore this puzzle-piece method was how those super-chic, skinny French people did it, it was enough for us.

We believed just as fiercely that Auntie Eva's personal dressmaker, Señora McClintock, would somehow take this mess of pinned tissues and turn it into breathtaking gowns for all of us, including the bride-to-be. The Señora, who, despite her last name, didn't speak a word of English, had given us today as the fabric-picking deadline.

Auntie Radmila had sweet-talked the owner of Stitsky's Fabrics into letting us "borrow" dozens of bolts of material. The entire living room was overtaken by huge swatches of shiny silks, gauzy chiffons, and heavily sequinned materials in only the most retina-searing colours. Everyone, including Mama who couldn't come today, had already chosen their fabrics and their patterns. I'd been so busy with basketball practices, games, hanging around with the Blondes, *and* the library, that this was the first time I had been able to come at all.

Far from being annoyed with me, as they had every reason to be, the Aunties were delighted.

"Ov course you vas busy," said Auntie Radmila, lighting up another cigarette. "You vas a busy, too popular girl. Is a very good ting. Ve are all very proud like za peaches."

"Ya!" agreed the other two.

Auntie Luba cupped my face in her hands. "How is it going vit your Papa?"

"Ya!" said Auntie Eva before I could answer. "Has he started drinking yet?"

I instantly decided that by "drinking" Auntie Eva must mean out-of-control, falling-down, police-at-the-door drinking as opposed to sneaking-a-couple-of-brandies-now-and-again drinking. I looked her straight in the eye and said, "No."

"Okay," Auntie Eva sighed. "You vouldn't say anyvay."

I opened my mouth to protest.

Auntie Eva wouldn't let me. "Ve know you like him." Dramatic sigh. "Ve vas just tinking about your poor Mama."

The Aunties nodded.

"And speaking of drinking, don't I get my one brandy?" I asked.

"Sorry, baby buboola." Auntie Eva shuffled off to find a shot glass and filled it to the brim with plum brandy.

Auntie Radmila patted my hand. "Ve vas tinking Mama is all za time vorking, vorking like she got ants in za pants."

Well, that was true. Mama kept explaining thoughtfully and calmly, right before she rushed out the door, that it was because Papa wasn't working. I knew it off by heart. She had to pay all the new extra bills plus the old legal bills, plus condominium charges, and so on.

I guess it made sense.

But it had the stink of punishment about it.

"Well," I shrugged. "At least she's not ricocheting from hysterical to catatonic, like all those nuts episodes she got into when Papa was still in prison, remember?"

"Zis is for true," they agreed, reluctantly.

Well, a point for Papa then.

"Okay, maybe von point," said Auntie Eva as she unfurled bolts of fabric over top of one another. "But your Mama is not nuts. On za von hands it vas a very, very difficult situation, on za ozer, she is, for sure, maybe strung a little bit too tight. And maybe, too, she is a little bit too sensitive in za head. And zen vit your Papa . . .," a perceptible wrinkling of her nose, "vit za prison, and za killing, but not really killing, and all zose moves, all zose stupid girls at za ozer schools, it vas too much for a too sensitive personality." She cupped my face in her beefy but perfectly groomed hand. "Tanks be to God, *you* don't have a sensitive bone in your body."

"Ya," they all nodded.

Wait a minute, wasn't it me who was tormented by "those stupid girls"? Besides, I could be sensitive.

If I put my mind to it.

I thought of my heroine, Ginny Brandon. She didn't have any sensitive bones either. Maybe when you were born, you were either dealt the "high-spirited" card or the "sensitive" card. But being *sensitive* sounded undeniably appealing.

Maybe, if I worked at it, like, made it a goal or something, it could be right up there with wanting to be a Blonde, hell, better. I made a note to discuss this with my diary, which I had not touched in weeks. I bet sensitive people write in their diaries every single night.

"Are you za leader of za Blondes yet?" asked Auntie Radmila sweetly.

The Aunties, God bless them, felt that I should be president of everything.

"No." I took a little swig of my brandy. "I could never be leader of the Blondes."

Much vigorous pshawing.

"For one thing, I'm not a Blonde."

More pshawing.

"And Madison, well, you know, she is the leader and always will be the lead Blonde. Besides, she was my best friend."

"You said 'vas.'" Auntie Luba poured herself another drink and dug into the pattern pile. "Here, zis von." She whipped out a Butterick pattern featuring a black halter-top gown with a slit down one side from mid-thigh to the ground.

"Wow," I said. "You think I can wear black?"

"Not za black," she tsked. "But za dress is very sophisti-cated and very good to find a boyfriend. Ve vill be having many young men at za reception." Auntie Luba winked at me.

I winked back, but I knew from past wedding experiences that "many young men" meant three guys in their forties and a bunch of eleven-year-olds.

"You did say 'vas.'" Auntie Eva was eyeing the pattern. "Luba, darling, sveetheart, you need breasts to put in a dress like zat. Za child still doesn't got none." She put on her glasses and examined my chest. "Okay, some, but not very many."

"Much," I said. "I don't have very *much.*"

"Is za same ting, much, many, you need more."

We all looked at my chest. Again. We'd spent a lot of time pondering my chest over the past couple of years. Certainly my breasts were better, a 32B, rather than a minus 32 from last year, but still . . .

"I meant 'is' of course. She *is* my best friend."

Auntie Eva raised an eyebrow at me.

"Really. It's just that, well, she won't tell the rest of them about the adoption and Edna. And the thing is, I've come clean, and we sort of absolutely promised that we'd both do it together, you know?"

When this did not garner the thunderous outrage on my behalf that I'd counted on, I played my trump card. "Plus, I think she's *ashamed* of Edna."

The Aunties pshawed, but I could tell their hearts weren't in it.

"Vat is she ashamed of?" Auntie Luba asked. "Eva, she should vear zis fabulous greatest new ting brassiere I saw it in za Simpson's last veek."

"Madison? Why would she . . .?"

"No, you." Auntie Luba came up behind me. "It is a totally space age to za moon brassiere vich can do halter. It's za best von yet, I promise. Not just padding. It takes za breasts and pushes zem together and up like zis."

And with that, Auntie Luba reached over in front and shoved my 32Bs up and pushed them together. "See?" she said triumphantly.

"Ya!"

"Oooo, zat's very, very good."

It was my own fault really. I may have accidentally mentioned a couple of hundred times that Alison Hoover, Luke's barnacle, was dragging around a pair of 36 double-Ds.

I looked down. I had to admit, they were pretty impressive shoved together like that. We had to buy the bra.

"Is she a very bad voman?" asked Auntie Radmila.

"Who?"

"Za secret grandma."

"Oh, Edna, no. But she's not like the Chandlers, you know?"

"No."

"Very proper, very high Anglican, fish forks at the table. You remember, I keep telling you about the fish forks."

"Oh."

"Edna just freaks out Madison. The way she looks, the way she talks and walks, and, to top it off, she has gas issues."

"Vell, oil crisis or no oil crisis," said Auntie Radmila, brandishing three different rolls of pink fabric. "She is za grandmama."

"No, not that kind of gas. I really like that middle pink, though. It's the *passing* gas kind of gas."

Blank faces all around.

"She farts a lot."

"Ohhh . . ."

"But she's just bonkers about Madison. Sometimes, Edna comes over for a few minutes on some flimsy excuse, just to look at Madison, and then she leaves, all happy just from a look, can you imagine?"

The Aunties nodded. They could imagine.

"And she's real fond of her rye and Cokes."

"She sounds like a lovely voman," pronounced Auntie Luba.

I felt righteous. "Yeah, so, see?"

Auntie Eva wrapped some fabric around my shoulders. "Ya, zis heated pink von is movie star perfect."

"Hot pink," I corrected.

"Zat is vat I said," she said. "And, Sophia, buboola, you for sure should be za leader of za Blondes, of everyting, but maybe for now you should also be giving some of your slack to Madison, no?"

Well, this was going nowhere.

"Huh?"

The Aunties nodded.

How do I explain this and still make myself really look good? I mean, Madison had left me twisting in the wind. Not only that but she kept prancing around acting like everything was the same as always.

Okay, well, so did I, but . . .

"Well, a bit of slack sure, but all I'm saying is that I came completely clean about all my secrets and all the lies and stuff, and besides, she *promised*."

"Sophie, za adoption, za farting gramma, za child is scared." Auntie Eva put her arm around me. "You did not have a choice, zey had to know. Even so za rest of za school still tinks your Papa is your Papa's brother, ya?"

"Well, yeah, but . . ."

It was official, this was going way wrong.

"Buboola," Auntie Eva shook her head. "Even ven you vas lying your brains out, you all za time knew who you vas, and *ve* knew who you vas, and you vas loved for who you vas, no matter who you vas."

"Uh, yeah . . . well, but . . ."

"Your Madison does not know who she is now."

"Ya!" Auntie Luba thumped the patterns. "Von minute she is full of blue blood and za next she is full of gas. Is a little confusing maybe for za child."

Well, that took the wind right out of my sails. "Yeah, well," I said lamely. Damn. I was going to have to work much harder on nurturing my "niceness" quotient along with that whole sensitivity thing. "Okay. And I really do like the heated pink fabric the best, Auntie Eva."

They all beamed at me.

Auntie Radmila fussed with my hair while Auntie Luba draped the slippery fabric over me.

"You vill be za most beautiful flower girl in za history of flower girls."

"Well, given that most of them are, like, four."

"No, no, no!" said Auntie Eva. "Just most beautiful, because you are most beautiful, end of za story." She lit another cigarette and waved it around for punctuation.

I kept eyeing all the tissue patterns and fabrics nervously.

"And *everybodies* vill see how beautiful at za vedding." Auntie Radmila raised her glass. Her eyes were twinkling. Something was up. We clinked our shot glasses.

As soon as I got home, I lugged out my diary. After careful experimentation with every writing implement we had in the condo, I discovered that the only thing that could handle Papa's beautifully textured handmade paper was Crayola crayons. Anything I wrote would look like the musings of an articulate six-year-old.

November 20, 1975

Dear Diary,
  Things to work on: inner beauty.
  How?
  Be more sensitive and nice.

But how? I needed a role model. I went back into my bedroom and rummaged through my romance carton. After

examining and discarding a couple of dozen possibilities
I settled on *the* one.

> *Instead of rereading* Sweet Savage Love *for the*
> *eightieth time, I will read* Nurse Ellen, *because she*
> *looks seriously nice and sensitive and full of inner*
> *beauty, so I'm bound to pick up a few pointers. And,*
> *besides, it was Madison's favourite of the Nurse*
> *books I lent her.*
>
> *Love,*
> *Sophie*

I read a few pages, groaned, and examined the cover
again. Nurse Ellen was looking downcast, clutching a bunch
of files to her chest. The copy under the title exclaimed:
"Love and a dedicated doctor don't always add up to
wedding bells—Ellen Burke had to show a nurse's courage
while knowing a woman's despair."

Eew, forget that. So instead of finishing the book, I called
up Sarah and harassed her as sensitively and nicely as I could
into promising that she would go to Planned Parenthood, right
after school on Monday. We didn't have practice on Mondays.
I said that I would go with her. I said that we had to do this
because I personally could not deal with the pressure any
more and it was screwing up my inner beauty.

After a lot of back and forth, pleading and sensitive threatening, Sarah finally agreed.

And I went to bed lovelier.

The Blondes all rolled into Mike's at about the same time
as the football team. The pretext was that we were all going
over to Kit's, right after my shift, to experiment with various
versions for our upcoming wedding hair. The reality was that
they wanted one good long last look at the team all together
and out of uniform, as the season came to a close. As soon as
the guys lumbered in, Madison started pouring coffee like she
does when we're all at Mike's during the weekdays, when I'm
not working. She did this perfectly, with efficiency and good
humour. In fact, Madison poured and moved through Mike's,
balancing saucers and smiles, better than I did.

I was the one who worked there.

Mike's was mine.

What can I say? It bugged me, which was not very sensitive or nice. My inner beauty was taking a beating.

On the other hand, my Luke sensitivity was operating at a fever pitch. Even though my back was to the restaurant because I was whipping up milkshakes, I could *feel* him coming toward the counter. It's pathetic. I am so hyperaware of Luke's movements in the restaurant that I know he's going to take a sip of coffee before he does. I sensed every step he took toward me. Only this time, rather than neatly stacking his plates on the counter, Luke would tear me away from the blender and do a page 373: *"His arm was clamped around her waist, and as her head fell back under the fury of his kiss she was suddenly, painfully aware of the hard, muscular promise of his body against hers."*

The rest of the team began filing out in dribs and drabs.

"Hey, Sophie." Luke sat down on the last counter stool rather than lining up for the cash register. "What's your badass posse doing here?" He turned to wink at the Blondes. They gave him a little wave back like it was an afterthought. God, they were good.

"Oh, uh," I said cleverly. "We're going over to Kit's to practise wedding hair, you know, for, uh . . .," I tilted my head toward Mike at the cash. "You know, the big wedding."

"Ahhh, the big wedding, yes. Speaking of the big wedding . . ."

Luke stood up. Jesus. All he has to do is stand up and I have a heart attack.

"Mike?"

"Yeah, kid?"

"Can I RSVP your invitation here or do I have to fill out that little card and send it back to you?"

Huh?

Mike snorted and stepped over to us. "Depends," he said. The cigarette that was attached to his lower lip had a good inch and a half of ash on it. It was my experience that those ashes rarely made it to an ashtray. "You coming or what? And, by the way, sorry that it's a single invite. My intended wants to keep it an intimate affair kind a thing."

So far they had received 357 acceptances.

"But my nephews George and Mike Jr. are coming stag too. You probably remember them. They were seniors when you were on the bantam team."

There was an undeniable flurry of activity at the Blonde booth. Mike's nephews played ball for Northern Heights a few years ago. They were legends. Jesus, the Aunties *had* actually come through with some young guys.

"Sure," nodded Luke. "Who doesn't? And yeah, I'm real honoured that you guys asked and . . .," he turned to me, "you couldn't keep me away."

Instant party in my heart.

"Good," shrugged Mike, cigarette still firmly attached to lip. "I'll let Luba know."

"Good," shrugged Luke. "I'll see all you guys there then," he said while paying up. Then he walked back to me, put his hands on the counter, and leaned in. "Don't let 'em mess with your hair, Soph. I love your hair."

And he left.

We all held our breath. Except for Mike, who kept looking from me to the Blondes and back. "So, did I do good? It was your Aunt Luba that insisted that we invite the guy and make it a single invite. Was that okay? It was her idea, you know, what do I know?"

We held our breath until the door shut.

"Like, I just do what I'm told, you know, what do I know?"

We still held our breath, as we watched Luke walk past the window.

"She said it would make ya happy, Sophie, that's what she said."

Madison darted over to the window, tracking Luke until he crossed over to the other corner.

And then turned back around and screamed, "YES!!!"

And then Sarah and Kit got up and screamed, "YES!"

Madison leapt over to the counter and grabbed me as hard as any Auntie would have. "He's yours, Sophie!"

Well, shame on me, again. A half a minute ago I was all pissy about her in my head and here she was being . . . well, just so Madison-like. I should have apologized, but that would've been confusing for all concerned.

"So, it's, like, a good thing?" said Mike, lighting up another cigarette.

We could barely hear him for all the squealing.

"Mike, are your nephews really, really coming stag?" yelled Kit.

"Yeah," he grunted. "The boys are coming . . . stag. Thank you, Mike, you did so good, Mike."

We swarmed him. "Thank you, Mike, you did so, so good, Mike!"

He pushed us away. "Ahhh, get out of my restaurant and go goof with your hair or whatever you brats were gonna do."

We flew out of there and onto the street. I was over the moon. Luke was going to the wedding. Luke LOVED my hair. Luke loved me. Luke would break up with Alison Hoover and give me his school ring. "Did I mention that Luke loved my hair?"

"Like, only seven times in the past two blocks, cupcake." Kit swatted my head.

"Hey! Watch the hair."

Sarah pulled me back behind Madison and Kit.

"It's all okay," she whispered.

"Okay!?" I said. "It's absolutely brilliant! And I'll help you with your hair, but no one is touching mine."

"No . . .," Sarah pulled me closer, "no, I meant with me. I don't have to go to the place where your library lady said."

"What? Oh no you don't! Sarah, you promised!"

Kit turned around.

"I want her to meet my miracle librarian, Mrs. Setterington. It's Sarah's only hope for . . . the . . . assignment." Kit turned back around.

"No, it's cool," Sarah whispered.

Well, how's that for sensitivity? I had vowed to keep my mind on Sarah's potential crisis on a non-stop basis until we knew what we were dealing with on Monday afternoon. Instead, I totally forgot about it and her, as soon as Madison started serving coffee and then Luke . . . Jesus, I didn't deserve to breathe.

"Sophie?" She tugged my arm. "Do you get it?"

"Sorry, sorry, what do you mean, cool?"

"I started in the middle of the night, a real mess too."

"Yay!" I threw my arms around her and squeezed just as Kit turned around. "Thank God, there is a God!"

"What's up, lovebirds?"

"Nothing, I mean, I did amazing on the assignment," said Sarah. "I don't have to see the librarian."

Kit looked at me, smiled, and raised an eyebrow. She didn't buy it for a second.

Sarah and I held on to each other all the way over to Kit's.

"I can't go through anything like this again," she whispered.

"Me either," I said.

"I am now, for sure, going to wait until I'm married to . . ."

"Me too," I said.

We swore over and over that absolutely no guy was worth that kind of grief.

Thing is, I didn't believe either of us.

We had boxes and boxes of hair paraphernalia to unpack at Kit's. We'd dropped off all the stuff two nights ago. Everyone had definite ideas about *her own* look and it all involved a variation of being dead straight, hence the equipment. Everyone also had portable hair dryers. I had bought one from my tip savings just for this occasion and now was not going to use it. We also had a vat of Dippity-do, bought by Madison's maid, Fabi, at the Toronto Barber and Beauty Supply store at Bay and Dundas, and dozens of empty frozen juice cans.

Sarah had a fair bit of wave to her shoulder-length hair. Prescription: Dippity-do, seven juice cans, and an hour under the dryer. Madison wanted straight, but with a flip out all around her face to highlight her new feathered hairstyle. Prescription: a whack of cans (the girl had a lot of hair) combined with different-sized rollers at the front, at least an hour under the dryer, and maybe touch-ups with a curling iron. We'd decide later. Kit had bone-straight hair but wanted to wear it in a puffed up half-ponytail. Prescription: Just a few juice cans and Dippity-do on top, half an hour under the dryer, and then vigorous teasing and backcombing to achieve the desired height.

It was serious business. The hair, once heavily Dippity-doed, was rolled around the cans, clipped in place, and then *very* carefully shoved into the plastic hair-dryer caps. It was a good thing I'd decided not to touch my rangy ringlets. We would have been there all day just with my mop. As it was, I was in major demand as an extra pair of hands running from dryer to dryer.

Kit was first out and we went over to the mirror to unroll and tease her up. "Everything cool with you, Soph?"

"Are you kidding?" I snorted. "It doesn't get better."

"Nothing you want to tell me? Remember, we promised. You sure you're not packing stuff you want to tell me about?"

I unrolled the cans with fairly steady hands. "No," I said. Just that Madison is hiding her low-rent biological grandmother from everyone, and Sarah is no longer a virgin, and you're seeing a therapist to keep a grip on your puking problem. Jesus, I wanted to lie down. These Blondes were killing me. "No, there's nothing, Kit, not my stuff. You got it all."

She sighed, got up and got a beer, and sat down again. "I know there's stuff floating around us, all of us. That's okay.

I just want us straight, you know?" She waved the can in front me, asking if I wanted one.

I shook my head. "We're straight, Kit. I've had it with secrets, speaking of which, are you ever . . .?"

"Yeah, yeah, yeah, I'm going to tell them, don't worry. I'm just not ready yet."

Yeah, well, maybe, when in God's name are we ever *ready* to tell that sort of stuff? I started backcombing, bit by bit. "Kit, you're okay, aren't you? Have you, do you still . . .?"

"No." She raised her self upright in the chair. "Just that once and it was the booze that time, I swear."

We looked at each other in the mirror. I nodded at her.

"And, and a couple of times last week when the divorce was finalized."

I dropped the comb. "Oh, Kit, I'm so sorry."

"S'okay." She examined her lap. "To be expected, under such exigent circumstances, as the shrink will no doubt say."

I still had such a hard time wrapping my head around the fact that it was Kit's mom who actually picked up and left. I mean, a *mom*. She was now an admissions officer at the University of Southern California, where Kit was expected to apply at the end of high school. Divorce was the next step, I guess, but . . .

"How's your dad?"

Small shrug. "I saw him drunk for the first time in my life last weekend. It was a combination funny/scary really. He passed out on the living room rug. I couldn't even get him up onto the couch." She was twirling an empty orange juice can.

"So . . . I just stuck a pillow under his head, covered him up, and left him there on the rug."

Drunk.

It came to me clear as anything, a full-blown epiphany: Kit's mother was totally responsible. She dumps the dad for no good reason and leaves the country. Of course he gets drunk. This kind of thing is *always* the mother's fault.

"Papa's drinking a bit."

Her eyes snapped up to mine in the mirror.

"Just a teeny bit, not at all like before, for sure." I started backcombing with more energy. "And I hide it, you know, I mean the evidence, just in case he's left a glass around or the bottle or hasn't washed it up clean enough. But it's not a problem and it won't be as long as Mama doesn't find out."

"Sophie . . ."

"Which is ironic, you know, because it's just occurred to me for the first time that she's probably the one who makes him drink."

Kit looked skeptical.

"Like how your mother made your dad get drunk, only more complicated. I can see it now." I was teasing her hair like I was possessed. "Papa's crazy about her, always was, you know? I remember that even from before. But she's so critical, so pushy, it's never enough, no matter what he does, no matter how hard he tries."

"Sophie, your mom has had a lot . . ."

"He's making her this table and she's going to hate it."

"What?"

"Doesn't matter." It was all so clear now. Why didn't I see it before? "It's basically all her fault, Kit. Papa is *so* sensitive, he has the soul of an artist and, like, she's always either at him *or* she's out the door. Did I mention that she's, like, never ever around?"

"I know, I've noticed."

"Like, what's he supposed to think?"

"Hey, Soph, your dad is great, but don't you think your mom . . ."

"Not that I mind. It's a bit of a relief really." I started spraying her. "I'm glad she's not around."

"Yeah, I know, Soph." She took the canister out of my hand. "I miss my mom, too."

"Miss her?" I returned to vigorous backcombing. "No, I don't, that's not what I'm saying."

"Right," she nodded. "Uh, I think we've got it high enough now."

I finally looked at her hair. "Yikes, sorry." Kit's half-ponytail was going to be good for an extra seven or eight inches. I smoothed her out and rescued the other two from their dryer bonnets. We continued fussing and primping for another hour. I even Dippity-doed my corkscrew curls. The Blondes insisted that this made them even shinier and blacker than before and, therefore, well, even more beautiful.

"Luke will flip," winked Kit.

"It's a damn shame we're only going to the basketball dinner tonight," said Sarah, surveying the results. Both the junior and senior teams were meeting at Attago Attwood's, the junior coach's house, for a "We'll Get Them Next Year" dinner. The juniors had done almost as badly as we had this year.

"What a waste," groaned Madison. "All women."

But it wasn't, not for me. What a day! The relief about Sarah, Luke coming to the wedding, Luke loving my hair. We all admired one another fiercely in the mirror. Come to think of it, there was a lot to admire.

When the blessed day of the blessed nuptials finally arrived, it was freezing. Didn't matter. We, the blessed bridal party, were a vision. It's always freezing in December in Toronto, but the Saturday of Auntie Luba's wedding was face-hurtin' cold. So, we were a frozen vision. No coats were allowed. The bridesmaids insisted. Coats would ruin all our grand entrances and, Lord knows, we had a lot of entrances to make.

The first was getting out of Auntie Luba's house. We stopped traffic filing into the limo. Auntie Luba's whole block came out to wave us on. They were in their parkas and snow-suits. Mike corralled a friend of a friend who ran a limousine service that catered to high school kids on prom nights, Pescatore's White Night Limos. Luigi Pescatore himself was our driver. The limo was also a vision. It was about three blocks long, all white and festooned with twinkling Christmas lights. To add to the overall sense of occasion, Mike, Luigi, and Papa sang Italian soccer fight songs all the way over to Old City Hall on Queen Street.

A small but significant crowd gathered around us as we disembarked. Auntie Eva, of course, felt compelled to greet people and thank them for coming. Shoppers and tourists clapped enthusiastically, drivers honked their horns, and their passengers waved. It was like the whole city was celebrating with us.

We certainly out-dazzled all the other wedding parties waiting in the dingy third-floor hallway in front of the Justice of the Peace's office. Of course, we were bigger than the other parties, what with me, Mama, Papa, Auntie Radmila, Auntie Eva, Auntie Luba, Mike, Mike's brother George, and the last-minute inclusion of Luigi, so that he wouldn't feel left out all by himself in the car. That and, well, we were just . . . bigger.

Our wedding appointment was for 4:30 P.M., to be followed immediately by a "full-blowing reception vit all za trimmings but very, very intimate for four hundred peoples" at the Hungarian Hall. I don't know about the hall, but we were wearing pretty well every "trimming" we owned. It made for a nice contrast with all the discreet beige and blue suits worn by the other couples waiting for their crack at the Justice, or the judge, or the mayor, or whoever was on the other side of the doorway at the end of the hall.

We "girls" had all slept over at Auntie Luba's so that we could get an early dawn start to hair, makeup, and a wake-up brandy. As a result, the bride was glorious, resplendent in a purpley, mauvey, silvery chiffon caftan. *Resplendent* is the exact right word too. I looked it up. It means "full of splendour and light." That was Auntie Luba, right down to her sparkly pink toenails. There was so much chiffon involved that you had no idea where the dress left off and Auntie Luba began. Pure genius when you come to think of it. The dress billowed and swayed every time she took a breath. The bridal bouquet held in her quivering hands was a giant globe of gardenias attached to a three-foot train of purple freesia and lily of the valley. Our wedding party smelled like a spilled bottle of Evening In Paris and Rothmans because the bridesmaids, the bride, the groom, and Papa were all smoking like chimneys.

Aside from being decked out in every substantial piece of jewellery they owned, Auntie Radmila and Auntie Eva were also perfectly coordinated, in extremely form-fitting aquamarine and silver brocade gowns. Their oil-drum bodies were so tightly girdled and trussed that I worried about how they were going to sit at the reception.

"Von does never sit at a reception, buboola." Auntie Eva patted my cheek. "It ruins za line, for sure. Beauty, little von, requires za stamina of an ox."

Then there were the four-inch silver lamé stiletto sandals that we all wore. My feet were throbbing already. Before I even thought to complain, Auntie Radmila was on me. "Von must never tink of von's feet—today, only beautiful tinking." More cheek patting.

Then there was the hair.

Even at their most casual, the Aunties believed in really, really big hair. They were convinced that it "balanced" them out. We all had our hair done by Señora McClintock starting at 4:45 A.M. The Señora worked like she was possessed, stacking beehive on top of beehive, and then adding whimsical flourishes like corkscrew tendrils the size of salamis. Each corkscrew looked as if it could be broken off and used as a weapon if things got too rowdy at the reception. The bridal party was thrilled with the outcome.

Mama, as the maid of honour, was breathtaking in her mauve and aquamarine chiffon, and even more breathtakingly—she was smiling. Papa and Mike looked lovely too. Mike was sporting a shiny black rented tux and ruffled shirt from the big and tall shop, and Papa had on his get-out-of-prison suit, which fit him better now. Mama had bought him a beautiful snowy white shirt and a silvery blue tie with a matching pocket handkerchief in keeping with the bridal colours. Everyone, including Mike, knew that none of the Aunties much liked Papa, but Mike had gone and made him an usher anyway. Poor Papa looked like he was going to crack under the pressure. Well, that and Mama had spent so much time at home all week that I know he didn't have much of an opportunity for a de-stressing snort of brandy.

Truth be told, I was pretty darned resplendent myself. I already had a head full of corkscrews, so the Señora just pinned a few back and up on my head with some butterfly rhinestone pins to give me a festive air and then shellacked the whole thing in place. But the dress, *my* dress, was a thing of wonder. It was a watery pink chiffon with a plunging neckline that gathered into an empire waist. The overall gloriousness, I must admit, was only made possible by Auntie's Luba's NASA-engineered "lift zem up and shove zem together" halter brassiere. My chest was an absolute showstopper, I mean, there they were. Right there. I noticed that Papa and Mike maintained tight eye contact with my forehead whenever they talked to me.

I, on the other hand, couldn't stop looking at them.

Is this what the other girls felt like every day?

All in all we were a profusion of giggling, sparkling, pastel glory, and clearly the envy of the entire third-floor hallway. At precisely 4:32, we were ushered into the Justice of the Peace's office, which looked disappointingly like, well, an office. The walls were an institutional grey and so was the Justice of the Peace, who seemed to become increasingly more nervous as we filed into his dingy little office.

No matter.

As soon as we all got in, it was transformed into a fantasy garden. I placed my bouquet at the bottom of his lectern thingy to pretty things up. Auntie Luba and Mama had let me pick out my own flowers. As a result, I had every bloom known to mankind stuffed into an arrangement that was bigger than most coffee tables. The bridal party showed approval of my gesture by collectively clutching at their chests.

There'd been a fair bit of chest clutching so far and it was early days yet.

The Justice cleared his throat several times, clearly overtaken by our high-octane glamorousness. "Good afternoon, my fellow citizens."

Mike took Auntie Luba's hand and kissed the tops of her fingers. "At last, my little gardenia, at last." Auntie Luba reached up and kissed the top of his balding head. Apparently, this was the cue for Auntie Eva to start wailing on the one side and for Auntie Radmila to start sobbing on the other. Even Luigi teared up.

The Justice of the Peace looked alarmed.

Papa kept patting and rechecking for the ring while trying to avoid the Aunties, which was a challenge in that broom closet of an office. Papa wasn't entirely sure of his official duties. Mike was a casual kind of guy. Mike's brother George was probably the best man. He was the brother after all. But on the other hand, Papa had the ring and in a pinch, since none of them were too sure about the ceremony, if the Justice asked who was going to give the bride away, irony of ironies, Papa was supposed to do the giving. "With pleasure," he had said with a straight face when Mike asked him about this contingency.

We were a room full of Europeans steeped in the elaborate tradition of either three-hour wedding services or two-minute quickies in the basement of the village's Communist Secretariat. None of us knew what to do in a Canadian office wedding. Picking the Justice of the Peace had been the most contentious decision of the whole wedding. Auntie Luba was Catholic, but Mike was divorced, so the Catholic stuff was out. On the other hand, Auntie Luba point-blank refused to convert to whatever religion Macedonians are, so Mike's church was out.

So here we all were, in an office.

Still, the service was lovely. The bridesmaids eventually got their crying down to a dull roar when they realized their makeup was at risk. Papa produced the ring at exactly the right time, if with trembling hands, and Mike and Auntie Luba did not take their eyes off each other.

We all knew, as sure as we were breathing, that when Mike and Auntie Luba were looking at each other, they did not see a tux from the big and tall store and a billowing caftan. Mike saw a trembling little nineteen-year-old in the outskirts of Budapest and Auntie Luba's eyes were filled with a dashing young resistance fighter. All the years, the marriages, the extra pounds were forgotten, made invisible. Everything else fell away. Our spell was broken only when the Justice said, with considerable relief, "You may now kiss the bride."

And Mike did.

Boy, did he.

The Aunties hooted and clapped. I hugged Luigi and George.

And Mike kissed her again.

And then again.

We all laughed and Mama started to cry.

And then Papa . . .

Papa stepped over to Mama, cupped her face in his hands, and kissed her eyelids.

I don't own the words to describe how I felt. I was soaring. I think we were all flying in that cramped, grey little office.

And Mike and Auntie Luba kept kissing like they'd never see each other again.

And I was hardly grossed out.

We all hugged the Justice several times while we waited for the paperwork to be completed. Then, after some heated discussion, Auntie Eva, Auntie Radmila, George, and Luigi settled in on a Croatian love song they mostly knew the words to. Mike held on to Auntie Luba while they swayed to the song and my Papa kept kissing my Mama's eyelids.

I can only pray that my wedding ceremony will be half as beautiful.

The receiving line took about two hours. Never mind your standard greetings:

Guest: "You look lovely."

Bride: "Why, thank you, and thank you for coming."

Long-winded, intimate, and intense conversations with everyone in the receiving line were the order of the day, punctuated by bear hugs and a fair bit of crying. We, the bridal party, stood in front of the head table and *received*. Everyone made their way up to us and then off to the bar, or first to the bar and then on to us with drinks in hand. The latter was trickier when it came to the hugging part. Mike and Auntie Luba were beaming. They were flanked by Mama, the best maid, and Papa, the maybe best man, then by Auntie Eva and George, who hadn't said a single word so far but who teared up on a fairly regular basis, then Auntie Radmila and Luigi, who was now, apparently, a formal member of the wedding party, and then, finally, me, the world's oldest and tallest flower girl.

We were dutifully, and sometimes passionately, kissed three times by every single guest who filed by. The Blondes went down the line like old pros, effusing about the gloriousness of the gowns, the handsomeness of the groomsmen, the splendour of the bride, and so on. Kit was turbocharged by the time she got to me. "Holy shit, Soph, you look great. Like the boobs! Did you know it was an open bar? We've all had two Southern Comfort and Cokes already!"

Madison smacked her in the shoulder. "Not to worry, we're going to start pacing ourselves in a minute, but she's right, Sophie, you look absolutely brilliant with breasts!"

"Hell, they're better than mine!" said Sarah, as she kissed me four times, but who's counting?

My Blondes.

The guest line wound down and around and even outside the hall. About forty minutes into this smoochfest, every hair on my body stood on end. The air electrified. Sure enough, five kissers down was Luke. Should I act surprised to see him?

"Why, Luke, what a surprise!"

No, he knew I knew he was invited.

Three kissers down.

Feign nonchalance?

"Oh, Luke, we are all so delighted that you could make it."

Two kissers down.

Jesus, who am I kidding? I'd be lucky if actual words came out.

One kisser away.

My whole body is pounding. Is it noticeable?

Then . . . "Sophie." He plants a kiss on my throbbing cheek. "Sophie, you're so . . ."

Next kiss, a beat longer on my left cheek. I am melting.

"What an awesome . . . you're so . . . can I have the first dance?"

Last kiss, soft, sweet, and cool, high on the cheek near the temple. My forehead is pulsing like a strobe light.

"No." I shook my head. I could feel each individually shellacked curl shaking in its own direction. "I mean you could, but you can't because it's the bride's dance." It felt weird, like each strand had a life of its own. I shook my head some more. "I hope you brought a lot of dollar bills."

Understandably he looked confused. I wanted to explain *and* bear his children, but a short, squat, sheep-herding-type man hustled Luke along, then grabbed me with gusto.

Finally, we were all seated at the head table and the first of the one hundred forty-seven courses was wheeled in and served by the perky Croatian catering crew. We brought them in all the way from Hamilton because the Aunties deemed these caterers "first class, lots of food, top of za notch, beautiful service and lots of food."

The speeches, hearty and heartfelt, were delivered mostly in English given the trans-European blend of the guests we had going on. People, well, Mike, Auntie Eva, Auntie Luba, Luigi, and one guy from table fifteen, got up between courses to toast the happy couple and offer their considered opinion on the whole thing.

Every few minutes throughout dinner, the hall would erupt in wineglass tinkling, thereby forcing the bride and groom to get up and kiss, which, I may hasten to add, the bride and groom seemed exceedingly happy to do. Once the Blondes got a hold of this little tradition, they were banging their forks against their wineglasses with the best of them, bursting with pleasure if they generated a fresh round of kissing. You couldn't help but notice them. They were so beautiful and so, so blonde, especially in this crowd. It was like a klieg light was shining over their table. Or maybe it was because Luke was there too.

Dinner wasn't over until 9:45 P.M.

And all through every single course and through each round of wineglass tinkling, I tracked Luke. Mike's very studly nephews were also at that table, as well as some seriously old guy who was attached to a semi-portable oxygen machine. They all looked like they were having such fun. Well, not the near-dead guy, but the rest of them. For a moment, I was sick with longing. Why couldn't I be at *that* table? I gave myself an immediate talking-to. How not-sensitive of me. But I still kept tracking Luke. I tracked him through the soup, the three salads, the cabbage rolls, the fried chicken and roasted veal, through the lamb on a spit and potatoes and through all the veggies.

And Luke tracked me too.

I tracked his tracking. He raised his wineglass to me at the end of the cabbage rolls and then took a sip. I raised my wineglass to him and then took a sip. And so it went for every single course.

I hate wine.

But I was pretty stoned by the time the wedding cake was rolled out.

Finally, it was time for the bride's dance. The musicians took their places on stage. The Zorbas, despite their name, were billed as a pan-European talent, equally "super-fantastic" in the Greek, Slavic, Italian, Hungarian, and Polish traditions. For their first big set piece, they were going to show off their modern Canadian hipness with a never-ending version of Engelbert Humperdinck's "Spanish Eyes."

The bride's dance, surprisingly enough, has nothing to do with the groom. This is no tender and tentative trot around the floor for the newlyweds with the rest of the wedding party eventually joining in. That comes later, much, much, later.

The first dance is strictly a cash money affair. For two dollars exact change, male or female, young or old, you get a chance to dance with the bride for a few minutes. I, as the world's tallest, oldest, and slightly stoned flower girl, was pressed into service. What happens is that the blushing bride stands in the very centre of the dance floor, while all the guests line up, then pay me their money, which I graciously place in my carnation-covered hamper. This allows the guest to take a swing around the room and have a few words with the bride before the next person cuts in and so on.

It all goes back to early village life. See, the intent was that, no matter how you did on the gifts overall and no matter how poor the newlyweds were, the bride and groom could leave their reception with the certainty that they could go home and immediately buy themselves a spanking new goat.

The Blondes thought this was beyond brilliant, bridge financing at its best. Needless to say, the dance goes on but forever.

And I loved every single minute of it. Sure, it was joyous and raucous and I like that kind of thing, but mainly I loved it because Luke kept lining up over and over again for more dances, even though he was clearly bewildered by all of it.

The first time he came up, he dropped in his two dollars and asked, "What's this all about, pretty flower girl?"

I fanned myself with three wilting carnations. "I do not know, kind sir. I'm a stranger here myself." I have *no* idea where that came from. All of a sudden I was channelling Scarlett O'Hara.

It must have been the wine.

I saw him trotting off to the bar to get change on several occasions. By the end of the bride's dance, Luke was into me for eighteen bucks and he was on fairly familiar terms with Auntie Luba.

Finally, it was time for the wedding dance. Mike bowed and took Auntie Luba's hand, and they swept across the floor to the "Anniversary Waltz," a king with his queen.

Oh how they danced . . .

Mike was shockingly graceful and fluid.

On the night they were wed . . .

Auntie Luba floated in his arms as light as lace, around and around, tears streaming down her face.

Then, after a few minutes, the probably best man raised the hand of the best maid, kissed it like it was the most natural thing in the world to do, and off they went. I'd never seen them dance before. My God. Papa was so strong and sure.

He moved with such powerful elegance. And Mama . . . Mama looked like she was born to be in his arms.

They were *that* beautiful.

My flower girl obligations were never-ending. It was understood that the bridal party is up for grabs, so to speak, by anyone who wants to grab them. The entire hall is encouraged to dance with them. I danced several polkas with twelve-year-old boys, waltzed with a procession of large, middle-aged men and older men with canes, and I participated in every Croatian *kola* there was.

The *kola* is a large, noisy, insane circular dance where you lock your arms around one another's backs and proceed with the steps at ever-increasing breakneck speeds. The object is to get as many in the circle completely airborne as possible. The best *kola* was when me and the Blondes and the female members of the wedding party were joined by the entire catering crew, including the kitchen and serving staff *and* all three bartenders. The mandolins and tamburas strummed faster and faster and faster. Our steps flew blindingly quicker until Madison, Kit, Sarah, and I all went airborne and stayed that way for the duration of the *kola* amid the guests' clapping and piercing calls of "yeeeeeeeeyah!"

When the music stopped, my head and heart were spinning.

And then Luke grabbed a hold of me.

"I've got you now and I'm not going to let anyone cut in." He pulled me close and wrapped me into him.

Jesus God.

The Zorbas, God bless them, decided to take things down a notch and launched into the Macedonian version of Elvis's

"Love Me Tender." Luke moved his left hand up, tight against the middle of my back, pressing it, pressing me closer. He took my right hand, placed it on top of his chest, and then covered my hand with his. It felt as if his heart was going to break out of his chest.

"Can you feel my heart?"

I nodded into his shirt.

"What am I going to do about that, about you, Sophie?"

It took everything I had, but I kept silent. A lifetime's struggle over crappy impulse control—mastered by Lucas Pearson's arms.

He sighed and, as impossible as it may have seemed, drew me into him even closer.

"You're so young."

What, I'm fifteen, he's eighteen. We're not talking Lolita here.

"I knew you were trouble the moment you crashed into me last year and your Snickers bars went flying."

I looked up at him. "Excuse me? You were the one who ran over me."

Luke smiled, exposing his lone dimple, then he reached back behind me and placed my head against his chest again. I inhaled the Ivory soap and maleness of him.

He kissed my hair. My knees would have buckled but he was holding on too tight.

Mr. Klempovitz, Mike's coffee supplier, was trying to cut in.

"Meet me outside," Luke whispered.

"I, uh, I can't, I'm supposed to be front and centre the whole time."

"At 11:30," his lips grazed my eye. "Even flower girls have to go to the john."

More urgent tapping on Luke's shoulder by Mr. Klempovitz.

"I promise, on my honour, that I'll have you back inside in five minutes."

Lining up behind Mr. Klempovitz was a nine-year-old boy and Mrs. Shlepka.

"Okay, 11:30, five minutes."

Luke pulled me tight and then let go of me. My arms were immediately filled by the overeager coffee supplier.

11:15, 11:20, and I was swung around the room by all manner of male and female guests. Just as I was going to beg off and collect myself before going out, Papa appeared before me. "Can a proud father have at least one dance with his Princess?"

"Oh, Papa." I hugged him. He was so handsome and clear-eyed and happy that I wanted to cry. We whirled around the room at a death-defying speed, but his grip on me was locked and secure. I'd never felt safer in my life.

"He is in love with you, this boy."

"Who?" I squeaked.

"Uh-uh, never kid a kidder, Sophia." Papa shook his head. "It was clear from the other side of the room. I know this feeling. I have it still for your mother. Yet," he looked away, "it's a hard thing for a father to watch."

If I could have blushed, I would have.

"I think that, well . . . I'm just crazy about him, Papa."

We slowed into a waltz. No one would dare try to cut in on the best man and the flower girl. It seemed that those who weren't dancing were watching us intently. I caught Madison being led around the floor by one of Mike's nephews, I couldn't sort out which was which, and Kit by the other. Sarah was cutting up the floor with a thirteen-year-old, a long line of preteens forming politely behind him.

Papa tilted up my chin with his finger and smiled at me. "Then, Princess, I can promise you, he'll be yours."

"But there's . . ."

"I promise."

The song came to an end and I excused myself to go to the bathroom. Papa kissed my forehead and smiled.

"Go," he said. He was still smiling and everything, but somehow . . . something . . . what?

Was he okay? A big part of me wanted to stay right there and keep dancing with my father. We would glide around the floor, waltz after waltz in this magic room that was sprinkled with miracles. I could make him happy. I have always been able to make Papa happy. It's what I do.

But the thing was, this time . . .

Luke was waiting.

"Go," Papa smiled.

I reached up and kissed his cheek.

He stroked my arm with the back of his fingers, still smiling. "Go," he said.

I pretended to head toward the ladies' room. My heart was pounding louder than the band's bass guitar. After casually checking to see whether anyone was watching, I made a casual sharp turn left and then casually skulked over to the emergency side exit. I knew from previous weddings that the exit had a small grille landing and iron steps leading down to the parking lot.

The cold air slapped me. Luke pulled me into him and then against the brick wall before I could exhale. He took my face into his hands. He was searching for something.

No words, just searching.

"Damn!" he said.

And then he kissed me.

Hard. Hungry.

The sharp rough ridges of the bricks bit into my bare back. He opened my mouth with his and I fell spiralling into a dark, warm tunnel.

That kiss was like nothing else.

I tasted the sweet saltiness of him.

We kissed on and on. It was like I was starving. I grabbed his hair and pulled him tighter.

Feeling like this was insane.

When he drew away, we were both shaking.

Luke traced the outline of my face, my neck, burning me with the back of his fingers. He looked confused and tender at the same time. "I . . . I've tried to break it off with Alison since the beginning of school."

He kissed my neck just below the ear, and I forgot to breathe. He kissed the hollow of my throat and took away all my words. "I was pretty sure . . .," kiss, "about you," kiss, "but," kiss, "damn, you're so young and so . . . oh God, Sophie." His voice was as rough as sandpaper.

Luke traced the outline of the halter, of my breasts. Jesus God. Tiny kisses fluttered further down my neck, between the plunging folds of the dress. His lips burned every spot they touched—an icy fire.

Why was my dress still on? What was it doing still on?

"But she got so crazy-needy, you know? It was scary."

Luke kissed my collarbone, gliding up my neck again and down. I could feel his eyelashes grazing my skin. His fingers tracing each curve of me . . .

All he has to do is unhook the little halter thing. . . . He outlined my straps, grazing, barely touching me.

I was prepared to burn in hell.

"I think I love you, Sophie." He cupped my face in one hand.

Love? I was spinning, it was like we were both whirling around on the landing. Love? He said . . .

"And I'm going to make a clean break of it with her right after Christmas. I don't want to, to hurt her as bad . . . but . . ."

His mouth on mine again.

I wrapped my arms around his waist, inside his suit jacket. His muscles shifted and strained against my hands.

Jesus God.

"Can you wait?"

"Wait?" I nodded. He didn't understand. Christmas? Two weeks? I'd waited for more than a year. Two weeks were nothing. I would wait for Lucas Pearson for the rest of my life. "I'll wait."

Then Luke put his hands on me and I just about lost consciousness.

He pulled back abruptly. Was he angry?

"You better go back in." Each word was ragged.

Go in? Where?

"We've been out here almost half an hour."

Right. The wedding.

I reached for the door handle, but my arms, no longer wrapped around him, drifted uselessly, the loss unbearable.

"Sophie?"

I turned around. Apparently words were still right out of the question.

He reached out and touched my face. "I promise."

He opened the door for me.

The laughter and the lights and the music crashed into me. I tried to adjust my eyes. I couldn't face the dance floor so

I drifted over to the corner nearest the bar. Everyone would know—surely they could see.

I smiled.

I couldn't stop smiling.

A group of men were singing Polish folk songs to the left of the bar. Papa was with them. He was singing too. I stopped floating just long enough to watch my father laugh mid-song. Mama was heading over from the other side of the hall behind him. But then, when I started toward him, as I stepped closer, I saw more clearly. *Oh, Papa.* He was holding a tumbler of brandy and ice. Mama wasn't there yet.

Jesus.

I stopped hovering, zeroed in on his hand, and picked up my pace. But Mama was closer, she was almost there. He wouldn't see her until it was too late. *Hide the glass!* The next few seconds unfolded in slow motion. Mama got to Papa first. Smiling and fresh, she looked like a girl as she reached for him. He stiffened. Then she saw. Hurt and surprise slammed across her face at exactly the same time.

Papa froze.

Out of nowhere, in the middle of all of this, Auntie Eva, larger than life, caught up to me, linked arms, and demanded to know where my "beautiful boy" was.

Then she saw.

Mama opening her mouth.

Papa seeing Mama. Papa disintegrating.

Auntie Eva let go of me and charged right up to Papa. She snatched the drink out of his hand. "Bless you, Slavko, darling." She took a sip. "Tell zem not so much ice za next time. Ice is for Canadians." She took another sip and made a face.

The colour had drained out of Papa's face. He and I were in a state of shock. Mama closed her mouth, put her arm through Papa's and smiled up at him.

Auntie Eva? Auntie Eva!? My head was spinning.

"You vant a sip, buboola?"

"Eva!" Mama admonished.

"Vat?" Auntie Eva said innocently. "It's practically vater!"

Mama waved her hand at her, whispered something, and pulled Papa back onto the dance floor. He laughed and swept her into his arms as if nothing had happened—had *almost* happened.

I grabbed the glass out of Auntie Eva's hand and knocked back a good gulp, then handed it back and gave her a great big brandy-soaked kiss. She responded with a bear hug. Between the control-top pantyhose, the girdle, and the midline bra— there wasn't an inch of Auntie Eva that you couldn't bounce a quarter off of. It was like hugging a satin tree trunk. She dragged me off to the dance floor and Auntie Eva and I tried our hand at a waltz.

We both led.

And somehow it worked.

Well, that just confirmed it. That whole day, the entire evening, hell, every single moment of Mike and Auntie Luba's wedding was bathed in a powerful magic.

Nothing would ever be the same again.

It couldn't be.

For the first time in my life I wanted to record it minute by minute, miracle by miracle, in my diary. Almost on cue, my Blondes toasted their glasses up at me from table seventeen.

They were having a ball. It was like I was one of them, but not, and this time it was okay.

I wasn't a Blonde.

And that was a-okay.

Right here, in the embrace of my unpredictably lunatic Auntie, dancing at my Auntie Luba's wedding and still wearing Lucas Pearson's kisses, at this moment, I was better than Blonde.

18

We didn't get home until dawn. I lay down for a couple of hours and then flew off to Kit's while Mama and Papa were still sleeping. Madison and Sarah had spent the night at Kit's and we'd made plans to rendezvous at ten in the morning for a full and frank debriefing.

The Blondes looked tired, hungover, and deliriously delighted with themselves.

I was the grand finale; so I had to sit through all the details of their evening before I could launch into my own personal *Sweet Savage Love* chapter out on the fire escape. I tried to concentrate, really I did, but it was like Luke's touch, his breath, was on this film loop that kept replaying non-stop in my head. Every so often, out of the blue, I'd shudder. No one noticed. They must have been secret shudders.

Not surprisingly, Madison and Kit scored big time with Mike's nephews. Talk about jailbait! Those guys were at least twenty! They were thrilled and nervous at the same time. "It's kind of freaky to have an old guy going after you," Kit admitted.

Sarah, who was still fairly fresh off of her university-man experience, kept quiet.

"However," said Madison, ever the master planner, "it's just the sort of thing that'll make our desirability quotient skyrocket at school." She smiled at Kit. "When it gets out, that is."

"Don't sweat, buttercup, it'll be leaked to Jessica by Monday afternoon."

Sarah, who'd sworn off men, at least until her period became more predictable, had had a brilliant time dancing and being fawned over by most of the male guests, young, old, married, single. She collected undying declarations of love from every other guy in the place. "It does a girl good to be flat-out adored, you know?"

I think I punctuated every new bit of information with a correct combination of "ohmygod!" or the all-purpose "I don't believe it!" coupled with a suitable gasp or sigh. But I was on remote control.

They droned on forever.

Finally, finally, finally—my turn. Within seconds, I had them on the edge of their beanbags. I made them feel the bite of the brick grooves on my bare back, the kisses on my collarbone, the urgency of his mouth pressing on mine. My stash of bodice rippers had nothing on me. I may have exaggerated just a teeny, tiny, little bit about how far Luke's hands explored. Not lies exactly, just a little creative licence. But it was pretty well the stroke-by-stroke truth. I had them swooning and panting on the shag rug.

"So, nothing until after Christmas?" said Kit. "That sucks."

Talk about killing the mood.

I nodded.

"Well, actually, that's pretty decent of him, when you come to think of it," said Madison. "He can't very well unload Alison during the holidays. They've been going out for almost two years. I mean, what's he going to do? Dump her and say 'Merry Christmas'?"

"Works for me," shrugged Kit.

"What this means," Madison continued, "is that Sophie is getting a really thoughtful and sensitive guy."

"Yeah," agreed Sarah, "and a major hunk."

"Well, it's going to take some doing to get rid of the barnacle, is all I'm saying," said Kit. "It may go right through the holidays. Brace yourself, Soph, I swear Alison knows something's up. That boy can't fart without her fanning him."

"Kit!" Madison swatted her.

"I'm just saying . . ."

While they bickered, I went right back to the landing with Luke. If he hadn't stopped, honestly, would I have? Will I? He's an "experienced" boy after all. He'll have expectations. Apparently I have expectations. And after he's broken up with Alison and we've been dating for a respectable amount of time, a month, say, well . . .

Bad to the bone.

And besides, there was a sexual revolution going on and increasingly it sounded like something I wanted to be a part of. And I loved him and he loved me. He said so. Not only that, Luke said that he loved me at first sight. Well, he said he knew I was "trouble" and that's pretty much the same thing.

And it's not like a thunderbolt comes out and strikes you dead right after. Look at Sarah. Then I cringed remembering the pregnancy panic.

But on the other hand, I would for sure go back to Mrs. Setterington, to get prepared properly. She wouldn't judge. Mrs. Setterington would just be there, like she always was. And she'd be there with serious, official information and maybe even some tips.

But then, on the *other* hand, how do you make it seem like you were just suddenly, totally, spontaneously, romantically, overtaken by the moment? The inescapable thing about preparation is that it makes you seem, well, *prepared*. None of the women in the romance novels were ever prepared.

But then again, on the other . . . okay, I was out of hands. You had to be an octopus to keep up with this argument. Thing is, Luke and I were going to have our children only *after* our wedding, which would be at the Hungarian Hall. I was definitely going to have to talk this whole thing out with the Blondes.

At some point.

I went home happy and horny. No, wait, I hate that word. I was *aroused*. That's so much better. Rosemary Rogers would approve.

I spent the next few days in a lovely Luke fog while I tried to cram for Christmas exams. Because we were on exam schedules, I rarely ever saw him or Alison in the halls. Which was good.

I guess.

I saw Mama a whole lot more though. She was home way more than usual. Christmas was a slow period in the real estate world. She threw herself into decorating, cooking, and baking for the holidays, while still leaving herself plenty of time to harass me non-stop about the quality and quantity of my studying. Yup, she was back.

Papa renewed his efforts to get a proper job but without much success. Apparently, Christmas was a slow period on the get a fantastic full-time Polish-to-English translating job front, too. Still, he was out every single day and sometimes the evenings too.

And I didn't clue in.

I was not vigilant enough.

I was so wrapped up in me and Luke and algebra that I missed the signs.

Exams ended on a Wednesday and me and the Blondes celebrated with our first annual cookie and gift exchange at Sarah's. It was great, I didn't think about Luke for minutes at a time. I didn't roll in until after ten. Mama was sitting in the living room by herself.

The TV wasn't on.

She was just sitting. Mama never, ever just *sat*.

"Hi, Mama, where's Papa?"

She smiled at the TV and patted the cushion beside her.

"Did you have a good time vit your friends?"

"Yeah, Mama, great. Look at all the cookies I brought back and they really loved your poppyseed ones. We're going to do it every year." She was looking right at me but not. "And, uh, we all exchanged our gifts. Madison was pretty Madison-like again. She has been since the wedding, I think." It was like I was talking to myself. "Maybe she's coming to a decision to tell everyone her stuff. I mean, Edna's going to be around during the holidays a fair bit, so . . ."

She stroked my hair.

"Yeah, and, uh, oh yeah, I think that Madison actually bought me one of those Instamatic cameras that I've been whining about, because the shape of the box is exactly right." Well, that and she said that she wanted me to take a lot of pictures of Luke. But I wasn't ready to talk to Mama about the Luke/Alison/me thing yet. Maybe when Papa got home, yeah, I could fill them both in. It was time for her to know.

Mama nodded and continued stroking my hair. We hadn't really been together like this since, well, since Papa had come home.

"And I know Sarah is going to be over the moon when she opens up the incense kit I bought her."

Mama kissed my forehead.

Yeah, it was time I told her.

"I didn't vant him to hurt you again. I vas so vorried, vaiting and vorried," she whispered. "I know how much you love him, Sophie."

Huh? She knew? How did she know? Well, maybe now that it's out in the open . . .

"I love him too, Sophie."

"What?"

"I do," she smiled. "But I vas so busy protecting me, dat I didn't protect you. I am ashamed." She looked away. "But da truth is, Sophie, I didn't know how."

What the *hell* were we talking about?

"Is all so complicated."

I'll say.

Before we could slide any further down this rabbit hole, Papa walked in.

"Ah! There they are! My beautiful, beautiful angels!"

He was beaming. He was happy. He was drunk.

Oh, not falling-on-the-floor drunk, but drunk.

"Good evening, beautiful princesseseses." Papa saluted the sofa.

There was no slipping this in under Mama's radar. We just sat there. I watched Papa out of the corner of my eye. I could just see him from where I was on the couch. Papa whistled and took himself to the kitchen, where we could hear him clattering away in the pots and pans drawer. Was he trying to make himself some coffee? Cupboard doors opened and didn't close. Taps turned on and didn't turn off. The coffee carafe was filled. The coffee carafe was dropped. Tea towels were extracted for the mopping up process. And then he started all over again.

The door above the fridge opened. It had its own peculiar little squeal. I heard him rummaging around and reaching way back. His favourite hiding spot. A glass fell into the sink, was retrieved, and . . . I couldn't take it any more. I got up and turned the TV on and sat right down beside Mama, who hadn't moved an inch.

She heard it too.

I thought I was being so smart, so sneaky, in hiding all of the traces. But what about all those times I wasn't here? All those sleepovers at Kit's or Sarah's, when I wasn't here to check, to make sure . . .

Jesus, Jesus, Jesus.

Mama knew.

She'd known all along.

We watched Irv Weinstein on the Buffalo news. There was a fire somewhere in Buffalo. There was always a fire somewhere in Buffalo. No one in Toronto can understand how the place is still standing.

Papa must've scalded himself with the hot water. Good-natured cursing and more clattering drowned out Irv for a couple of minutes. I wanted to find a nice Doris Day movie or Johnny Carson, but I couldn't move to change the channel.

He pulled out a kitchen chair and seated himself with a groan.

Or I could turn up the sound really loud.

But I just couldn't move.

Then Papa started talking to himself. Except that it sounded like he was having this whole big conversation with someone, someone who wasn't there. He wasn't just muttering or slurring to himself. He was *talking*. There were long pauses followed by hearty retorts and vigorous "da, da, das." I didn't know what the conversation was about. Papa was talking to his imaginary friend mainly in Polish.

A glass tipped over on the table, more good-natured cursing. The glass was refilled. It sounded as if he was reassuring someone.

Mama took my hand in hers and squeezed it. We were now on to Buffalo's weather forecast, lots of snow. Buffalo was definitely going to have a white Christmas.

The conversation in the kitchen started to get a little heated.

Apparently, they were having an argument.

I turned to Mama, who was immobile and staring at the sportscaster now. The Buffalo Sabres were actually doing really well this season. She wasn't even blinking. How could I have thought that she wouldn't have put the pieces together? Mama had been on high alert just as I had. What was I thinking? Why didn't she say anything? Why didn't I?

And then Papa started to cry.

And then it escalated.

Papa was racked with sobs, but he kept choking out "Why?" over and over again.

Mama winced.

Why what, Papa?

He cried right through the end of the news and into the feature film. I sat holding Mama's hand and listening with my whole body, straining to hear.

"Why? Why?"

I'll ask him what that was about tomorrow. Then I remembered. I was eight all over again. I remembered that Papa never remembers.

The universe shifted. I got up. "I'll take care of him, Mama."

She looked up at me. "No, Sophie, it's too . . ."

"I want to, Mama. It's okay."

She shut her eyes. "Thank you," she whispered.

I made my way over to the kitchen. Papa was slumped on the table, convulsing with sobs. I remembered that too. I touched his shoulder and gently got him up. It was easy, really. There was no trouble leading him out of the kitchen and into their bedroom. Somewhere, in between taking his jacket and shoes off, Papa stopped crying. For a second, it seemed that he saw me clearly and patted my head.

"Sophia," he said. "My little princess, you're here."

"Yes, Papa, I'm here."

He tried to pat my cheek, missed, and just waved his hand in front of my face.

"You are always here for your Papa."

"Yes, Papa," I said.

And I put my father to bed.

19

Papa was on his very best behaviour through the rest of the holidays.

Mostly.

Christmas dinner was held at Auntie Luba's. Auntie Luba and Mike prepared our traditional feast: roast pork, roast lamb, schnitzel, cabbage rolls, and turkey. The turkey was basically just for show, a nod to the country that had adopted us all. None of us much liked turkey and were extremely suspicious of anything to do with cranberries, but we'd feel guilty somehow if it weren't there on the crowded table. Mama was on the lookout for a new house for the newlyweds near the restaurant, but until then, Mike had reluctantly moved into Auntie Luba's old house, muttering all the while about it being haunted by Uncle Boris's cheap aftershave.

The entire wedding party was reassembled for the dinner, including Luigi, who, it appeared, was now more or less part of our family. Since the wedding, it was painfully obvious to absolutely everyone that Luigi had a major thing for the much-married Auntie Eva. For her part, Auntie Eva remained stubbornly resistant to Luigi's charms. Actually, she barely acknowledged his existence. Maybe it was the four divorces thing.

I don't know how it happened, but somehow after the wedding, I stopped being completely grossed out by the idea of old people having those kinds of "feelings" for each other. Hell, I thought it was kind of cute; so I kept talking him up. "Come on, Auntie Eva, put him out of his misery. He's adorable." Luigi was ogling her from the other side of the Christmas tree. "Okay, so he's a little shorter than you, but . . ."

"Pleez, buboola," she sniffed. "He's a taxi driver."

"No, Auntie Eva, he owns a fleet of limousines."

"Zat is vat I said," she paused. "Vat is a fleet anyvay? More zen von taxi? How many taxi cars iz he having exactly?"

"Limousines, Auntie Eva. Luigi has lots and lots of limousines."

She eyed him critically across the room. "Vell, maybe, if you put him in a suit zat is not made from polyester . . ."

Papa didn't drink that night.

And I didn't hear from Luke.

Of course.

That was our pact. I understood that. We'd be together *after* the holidays.

The Blondes all went away right after Christmas. Sarah and her family went to West Palm Beach every year on Boxing Day. Kit was spending the holidays with her mom in California. Madison's family all decamped to their ski chalet in the Georgian Peaks. The Chandlers tried to get me to come—I could rent skis, they'd arrange for lessons, and so on but I begged off. I said I had a pathological fear of ski boots.

I was right back to lying my face off.

Maybe I should write all of this down in my diary.

Or not.

The stupid diary was only ramping up my free-floating anxiety. It had begun to feel like an end-of-term paper hounding me, reminding me that I hadn't even started the research and now I was so pathetically behind that I might as well not hand it in. I was flunking "diary."

Thing is, I had to stay home to keep an eye on Papa. It's a pretty vague job description, but it's full-time. I don't know how this works, but somehow, I felt like the guilty one. My nerves were shot. It was like I was holding up an airplane. I kept waiting for something to happen—actually to *almost* happen, but this time I'd be there to fix it *before* it happened. By the time Kit called from California, I unravelled.

"Hey, rosebud, how's it hanging?"

I managed a "hello" and "great" before bursting into tears. I cried and then I apologized for crying for very many expensive long-distance minutes. Somehow, in there, I conveyed that it wasn't anything to do with Luke.

"Your old man?" she asked. "How's your father doing, Sophie?"

"Good, mainly."

"Sophie?"

"Okay, he's kind of drinking out in the open now, some-times, I mean."

"Shit," she said.

"No, no," I said. "In a way that's not so bad. I don't have the pressure of double-checking him and making sure he's hidden everything and everything. And . . . he never gets really smashed. I'm watching him, real hard, and it's not like he's having conversations with himself."

"What?"

"Nothing. He just gets a little buzzed now and then. You'd hardly even know and Mama's not all over him or crazy even. We don't talk about it. It's like everything is normal, except her nails are such a mess."

"Her nails? Soph, you are so not making any sense. You're not bent out of shape about her nails, are ya? What *is* the problem, Sophie?"

"I don't know!" I wailed. "I'm going mental. It's, it's, like when they tell you a hurricane is coming, prepare, prepare, and you're all prepared but you don't know for what. You're just waiting and waiting for the damn hurricane, you know?"

"Well, no, but that was a pretty impressive analogy and a nice use of repetition."

"Kit!"

"I bet you did really well on your English exam, espe-cially on the literary terminology section. I think I blew the big one on that."

"Kit, what the hell?"

"There, you stopped crying, didn't you?"

Right. She was right. Between hiccups we eventually decided that I wasn't going to try to keep my worries about Papa under wraps this time.

"Look, if it makes it easier, I'll spill on the puking. Ooops, bad word choice."

"Yeah, okay," I said. But I wasn't going to hold my breath. I'd been down that road before with Madison. The Blondes just couldn't seem to cough up their end of secret spilling. Well, that was them, this was me—secrets sucked. I said I'd lay it out as soon as we all got together that first weekend after school started. "But it's not like they're going to know what to do." It was a last-gasp whine on my part.

"It doesn't matter, Soph. We're *friends,* remember? You'll feel better just having talked it through and maybe I will too."

I didn't ask her a single thing about California, her mom, was she puking, how was it going, nothing.

Jesus, I suck as your basic breathing human, let alone a "nice" or "sensitive" one.

Somehow, I got through the rest of the holidays. Auntie Eva took us out with her and Auntie Radmila to a "super-duper too fantastic" New Year's Eve dinner cabaret performance at the Royal York Hotel. Auntie Eva wouldn't hear of letting Luigi come. She said she was playing hard to get, which implies that she was "gettable," so things were actually looking up for Luigi.

The Royal York is a very glam kind of place. It's where the Queen stays when she wants to hang out in Toronto. We all dressed up in our wedding outfits again. We were the only people there under ninety. The Aunties said it made them feel like "spring kittens." If Luke and I were a "Luke and I," we'd be at some crazy-mad party rocking out together in a corner. Our song would be playing. Note to self, must find an "our" song.

I sure wasn't going to find it that night. There was a band with trombones and a Moog synthesizer and some guy singing Frank Sinatra songs non-stop.

Next New Year's Eve, *next* New Year's Eve it would all be so incredibly . . . but *this* New Year's Eve, I was at a round table with napkins that were shaped like swans, with my parents and the Aunties, eating dry roast beef and keeping tabs on Papa. The one bright spot was that, since Papa was the only guy, he had to dance with all of us ladies all night long. Auntie Radmila and Auntie Eva kept hauling him back to the dance floor each time he'd return with either Mama or me. They were relentless. They were amazing. Papa barely had time to catch his breath, let alone get drunk.

I should have noticed before.

I wasn't alone.

Mama and the Aunties were preparing for hurricanes too.

20

The first day back at school was a Monday. I was sure that Luke would call on the Sunday night. I mean, about where to meet up so we could talk and everything. I was afraid to pee for fear I'd miss his call. Then right after dinner, Mama called Auntie Eva and chewed up almost seventeen minutes of valuable Luke-trying-to-get-through-to-me time. I don't know why I was sure he'd call. He didn't have my phone number. Hell, he didn't even know where I lived. And besides, there was probably just way too much to say on the phone, after all.

It must have been awful. Alison probably went nuclear on him, and then hysterical, and then ballistic. Someone like Alison, someone who wore that much eye makeup, would pull every trick in the book. I bet it was ugly. The poor guy.

I spent the whole day racing from the end of my classes to the end of Luke's, hoping to catch him. I'd memorized his schedule way back in September and knew it better than my own. I didn't even stop for lunch. Luke was never where he was supposed to be. I raced from class to class, from gym to cafeteria. I trolled the school all through lunch period. What the hell? By the end of fifth period, I was panicked and foggy at the same time.

He must be sick.

Jesus, that's it! Maybe he'd been sick through the whole holidays even. And that's why he didn't call after Christmas or New Year's or last night!

My poor sweet Luke was racked with pneumonia and probably in an oxygen tent while I selfishly went tearing around the school with my heart in my hand. On the off chance that he wasn't in intensive care, I roared up to the physics lab on the third floor. It was his last class of the day. I took the stairs two at a time and made it just as the class was breaking up. Everyone streamed out in twos and threes, then one by one, and then finally, Mr. Parker, the physics teacher.

No Luke.

Where else could I check? The halls were empty. It was like a tomb up there. I was still trying to catch my breath when I saw Kit running toward me, full-on *running*.

"Sophie! My God, Sophie!"

She caught up to me and grabbed my arm.

"Have you heard? You haven't heard, have you?"

I shook my head. We were both out of breath.

"I've been trying to find you all afternoon. Where the hell have you been all day?"

"What? Heard what?"

"Sophie, oh shit!" Her eyes were wet.

"What! What!" I was vibrating.

"Sophie, oh my God, Sophie, she's pregnant!"

"No way! Not possible!" I exploded. "Sarah *said* that she started her . . ."

Kit's face contorted. "Sarah?" Then she softened and took a hold of both my arms. "Sarah? Hell no, Soph. It's Alison, Alison Hoover is three-months pregnant!"

My head filled with water.

"Luke?" I whispered.

"That's right, sweetie, Luke got Alison pregnant. It's all through the school." Kit grabbed on tighter. "Oh God, Sophie, I am so, so sorry. Men are dogs."

She gripped me tighter as I started to sway. Alison?

"But he loves me." I said it like the mere saying of it would change everything, undo and obliterate every one of her words. "He said so, he did. He promi—"

Kit stepped back but still held on to me. "Sophie, look at me, Sophie."

It was like listening to someone under water.

"Sophie, babe, they're going to get married in the next couple of weeks."

"Married?"

"Well, yeah, see, there's the baby, and, well, he, Luke is going to do the right thing."

"The right thing?" *I'm* the right thing.

"Hey, don't get me wrong, I know the bitch planned this. She knew she was losing him at the beginning of the school year. You got to hand it to her . . ."

Blah, blah, blah, blah.

"He said . . ."

"There's going to be a baby, Soph. He was sucker-punched."

It was so cold. Did they turn off the heat at 3:30 or something?

Kit took my arm and tried to pull me forward. "Come on, kid, I'll take you home."

"No!"

I startled the both of us.

"Sorry, I, no . . . I have to go down to my locker and . . ." *And what?* I wondered.

"I'll go with you, do whatever."

I didn't budge.

"Look, Soph, you can't be alone, you need . . ."

"I'm fine, Kit, please. Please."

There was no expression on her face. "Yeah?"

"Okay, uh, that's a big hairy lie."

She nodded.

"But I'm not going to do anything stupid or melodramatic. You have my word, Kit. I just need a little bit, some time to, uh, Jesus . . . uh . . ."

"Take it in?"

"Yeah, thanks. I will call you tonight at some point, even if it's at midnight, even if I just say I'm okay or . . . not."

"So what, you're going to stay at the school by yourself?"

"Just for a bit. Please, Kit, please, I really, really need to be alone." Still no movement. "Sometimes *friends* need to be alone."

"Okay, I . . . maybe, I guess." She hesitated. "But if you don't call, I'm going to start calling by ten and keep on calling until I get you, or I make you all mental, understand?"

I nodded. I think.

Kit walked away very, very slowly. When she was almost at the end of the hall, she turned around and called out, "I love ya, Soph."

I waved.

Yeah, yeah, yeah.

Everybody loves me.

I made my way around the corner and across the empty main corridor to get to Luke's locker. When I found it, I slumped against it hard. The steel was cold. The little air vents bit into my back.

Pregnant?

I don't know how long I'd been standing there in a coma when I heard the footsteps. Probably the janitor. How embarrassing. He'd want to know what I was doing there. None of the winter teams had started up yet. I could maybe tell him that, uh, that . . . but then the hairs on my arms stood on end.

"Sophie."

He was in front of me in a heartbeat.

"Sophie, I was waiting for you downstairs by your locker all this time."

His eyes were bloodshot and swollen. He'd been crying.

My Luke.

I could take him in my arms and comfort him and tell him it would all be okay.

"Sophie," he whispered. He reached for my face and closed his eyes. Luke's lashes were so long and dark that they seemed to be tangled in tears. He touched me.

And I punched him.

It was like hitting a wall. Luke gasped and I hit him again, and then again. He let me pound and hit until I couldn't lift my hand any more. Then he took me in his arms, grabbed my head with his hand, and placed it on his chest. I inhaled him one more time. My Luke.

We both started crying. What a sight, Lucas Pearson and me, crying in the third-floor corridor of Northern Heights.

He cupped my face in his hands and kissed my soaking eyes. "I do love you, Sophie. I'm so, so . . . oh God."

Then he let go.

Turned.

And walked away.

I hadn't said a single thing. Again.

I slumped against the locker and slid down to the floor.

Just to collect myself. There were pieces of me floating all around the school.

Was it all a dream?

Which part?

I would have slept with him. Yeah, yeah, I would have, I think.

I started to shake. It was so, so cold.

I didn't know what else to do. What to think, where to go.

I was lost.

I sat shivering and shaking under Luke Pearson's locker for almost two hours before I finally got up to go. Enough. Enough already.

I have a home. Mama was waiting.

It was time to go home to my Mama.

In the end, I didn't get home until after eight. I spent all that time crying my fool eyes out in the third-floor corridor. Every time I tried to get up and go, I'd get a few steps under me and then a fresh wave would roll over me. I'd have to sit down and cry some more. It was like I couldn't walk and cry at the same time.

By the time I got to the condo elevator, I wasn't so much dry as a bone as I was hollow. My insides echoed.

Apparently, they had mobilized in minutes.

Auntie Eva was manning the phone. Auntie Radmila was just bundling herself off to the Italian café on College Street. Auntie Luba and Mike were already on the road. Mama was pacing.

"Buboola!" Auntie Eva slammed down the receiver. "Tanks be to God. Ver vas you, sveetie, baby?"

Okay, this was a bit excessive for being a couple of hours late. I could have been with one of the Blondes or . . .

Mama came to a full stop in front of me. Her eyes were muddy.

What the . . .

"Papa is not home."

I looked at my watch, 8:50 P.M. "Okay, well, I mean, did he miss dinner or something? It's not even nine . . ."

She hugged me. "Sophia . . ."

Sophia? The air got thick and soupy. Mama *always* remembers to call me Sophie. I stepped out of her arms.

"He did not come home last night, like da last time."

The last time?

I understood immediately.

I vaguely remembered that there were other times, binges other than "the last time," maybe lots of them. But I clearly remembered the *last time,* the night of the bar fight. The Aunties flying off in all directions, the searching, the calling, the drives down Bathurst Street and College Street. I was left at home to man the phone. I didn't go to school and . . .

Jesus.

We didn't hear until two days later that Papa was in jail and charged with manslaughter.

I scanned the condo. The Aunties were in overdrive. Different apartment, same players. Auntie Eva manning the phone, calling the hospitals, and muttering between phone calls. "If he is not dead, I am going to kill him for sure!"

Auntie Luba driving around, going from bar to bar.

Mama silent and in manic pacing mode.

I became the "murderer's kid" the last time.

But that was then.

Not again.

I filled up.

I needed reinforcements. Kit was up to speed on the whole Papa situation. But Sarah was the most sympathetic, but then again, Kit had her licence. "Auntie Eva, I need the phone for a second." She grudgingly handed it over.

Even though I must have dialled her number, I was stunned to hear her voice.

"Hello?"

"Madison? Madison, it's Sophie, I need help." And then, amazingly, I started to cry again, oh not the snot-slobbering sobs like back at Northern, little tears. They were all I had left. The words tumbled and tripped over each other, "didn't come home," "no, last time," "don't know," "yeah, when he was arrested," "don't know."

"Meet me down in your lobby in ten minutes," she said.

I put down the receiver and told everyone that Madison was coming.

Auntie Eva snatched back the phone. She still had three hospitals to go and then she'd start in on her list of police precincts. Apparently, Luigi was on his way from dropping off a couple of honeymooners at Niagara Falls. His marching orders were to concentrate on the corridor of bars near the Hungarian Hall. Mama came to life and started rooting around for the names and phone numbers of all of Papa's old drinking buddies, whom he had promised to never ever see again. I fessed up about Želko and the secret dining table project. She grimly added Želko's last known numbers to the growing pile in front of Auntie Eva.

Every hour, on the hour, the outgoing calls were to be stopped to allow for a fifteen-minute check-in period of incoming calls. Our kitchen looked like the control centre for the North American Air Defense Command.

My stomach helicoptered. I couldn't be there one single second longer. "I'm going to wait for Madison in the lobby."

Mama walked me to the door and kissed my forehead. "It vill all be fine," she lied. She tried to hug me, but I dodged her.

I'd had it with being hugged.

Madison was already there in the lobby, pacing.

"How did you get here so quick?"

"I drove." She started toward me.

Jesus, she was going to hug me too.

I shot out both my arms. "Nothing personal, but I can't take one more hug. What do you mean you drove?" I looked outside and into the family's Mercedes. No one there. "Madison, you don't drive!"

"I almost have my temporary." She looked indignant.

"Your parents are going to kill you."

She shrugged.

"And what if we get stopped by the cops?"

"Grandfather is a judge, remember?"

"Okay, it's your ass."

Well, it was mine too. It was freezing rain outside. The walkway was slick. This was nuts. But then the doors to the Mercedes shut with such a comforting, heavy thud that I calmed down for a minute. It would be like driving around in a Sherman tank. Madison was a good driver, I thought. Not that I'd ever been in a car with her, but you know, her being Madison and all.

We both inhaled together.

"It's a little icy on the road." She put the key in the ignition. Her hand shook, but just a little. "We'll go real slow." She turned on the car.

We exhaled.

"Look, Soph, before we head out," she went for the clutch, "I am insane about the Luke, uh, situation thing. But I'm here for you about that and about whatever this is about Papa. Anything, Sophie."

Jesus, Luke.

The brilliant thing about having several bone-crushing crises in your life at the same time is that, apparently, you can only hold on to one at a time. Luke? I'd have to table being suicidal about Luke for later. Her hand was still on the shift.

"AND I am so, so sorry for being such a pig."

"Huh?"

She nodded. "That last part is by way of an apology."

"Madison, Jesus, you don't have to . . ."

"Oh yes, I do, Sophie. I don't want you to think I don't know. Thing is, I'm not much of a driver and there's an ice storm out there. I'm not going anywhere with this crap between us." She stared at the mileage watchamacallit like she expected it to read something other than zero. "You tried to get me straight on how secrets suck the life out of you and I didn't listen. Worse, I promised you I'd come clean and then I bailed."

I started to say something but she put her hand up.

"No. Let me get this out, we've got to go."

She took a big breath. I took a big breath. We fogged up the car. I started wiping the windows with my mitten.

"I *know* I shouldn't be ashamed of being adopted, of, of, well, Edna. But I am. Every time someone makes a crack about my *blue blood,* I just want to . . . anyway, if it makes it any better, I'm really ashamed that I'm ashamed."

I stopped wiping and looked at her.

She was babbling. I know from babbling. This could go on for hours.

"But mainly, I'm mainly ashamed that I lied to you. I lied just like . . ."

I put my hand on top of hers on the gear shift. "Madison, I love you to pieces, but right now, I don't give a damn about any of that."

"Right," she nodded. "What am I doing? Sorry. I don't know what's the matter with me."

"Start driving, Madison."

"Right. Where are we going?"

"Don't know. If we ever make it out of the turning circle, I hope to get inspired."

"Right," she said.

We crawled a few inches.

"Oh, and I should also tell you that I called Sarah and Kit. They're combing the bars along the Bloor subway line."

Now, that sounded more like my Madison. She'd mobilized the troops.

She stopped the car again. Jesus, we hadn't even made it out of the driveway. "We had a little meeting at Mike's right after school, before all this happened."

"About me!?"

"Yeah, mainly. We were all freaked about the Luke thing."

Okay, was I going to have to drive the damn car myself?

"Sophie, I know it all, about Sarah's almost pregnancy, about Kit's thing with the puking. And I swear, Sophie, I'm going to tell them about me as soon as this is all over."

Jesus, what a group we were. All of a sudden, I wanted to crawl in the back seat and take a nap. Madison could wake me up when this was all over.

"And that's a promise."

I'd come to hate that word. You think it means something, this "for sure" thing. It only means that in the romance novels. In the real world, in *my* world, *promise* is the shady lady of the English language.

I must have nodded my head or something, because, Praise the Lord, she finally shifted into gear.

I started wiping furiously with both mittens again. You could barely see out the front window. "Shouldn't a fancy pants car like this have some kind of sucking machine? I'm sure your mother doesn't keep a spare mitten on her for foggy nights."

"I don't know." She bit her lip. "I've just driven the instructor's Toyota."

Jesus God.

While Madison drove, I turned and punched every button and knob in sight. Happily, I turned on the headlights in the process. That gave us pause. We both thought that the lights were on already. I got the radio on and off several times, figured out all the automatic windows, and got the temperature up so high, we could've defrosted a turkey. Finally, finally, I hit something that turned on the fan full blast. It sounded like we were at the airport, but at least we could see, so I wouldn't let Madison touch it. Even with the fan, we could still hear the ice pellets attacking the car. What were we doing?

"So?" she yelled.

"So what?" I yelled back.

"Are we good? Do you *believe* me?"

I believed that she'd stop the car again if I didn't answer. Madison was sitting ramrod straight. Her hands were glued to the steering wheel and she was breathing in time to the windshield wipers. I shook my head. I used to wish that I *were* Madison. I wished it so much that at times I was blinded by the sheer want of it. And here we were, she was as scared as I was.

What did I believe? I believed that my main Blonde was back and that all that other stuff, the telling or not telling . . . none of that mattered.

Her hands were trembling on the wheel.

"I believe you," I yelled.

"Well good, okay, then," she yelled back. She stared forward and leaned toward the windshield. "Let's find your father."

We rolled onto Mount Pleasant Road and then Eglinton Avenue—very, very slowly. It was a mess out there. Cars were skidding and fishtailing all over the place.

Neither of us had a plan really, other than to find Papa, to not crash into anything, and to not get stopped by the cops. After an hour and a half of driving up and down Eglinton and hitting all the Duke-of-Something-or-other pubs, I called in to NORAD kitchen control from a pay phone.

Nobody had spotted Papa. Kit and Sarah called in at about 11:15 and were given the requisite time/call procedure. I swore to Auntie Eva that we'd be back by midnight, whether we found him or not. She was beside herself on the phone. Not about Papa. It had finally dawned on her that Madison and I were "out zere" driving around in the freezing rain.

"You vill break your neck to pieces looking for zat bum. No offence, I know you like him."

And that was without her knowing that my chauffeur only had her temporary licence and had never driven anywhere other than the Yorkdale Shopping Centre parking lot.

We were inching along Yonge Street when Madison burst out, "Fran's, let's go to Fran's."

"You want a burger?"

"No, but it's open twenty-four hours. We had such a nice lunch there, remember? Back in September with your dad, you, me, Kit, and Sarah, and Luke came by?"

I winced.

"Sorry, sorry. I mean, it was a good time, one of those good memory kind of deals, and Fran's is licensed, right?"

"Yeah, maybe," I nodded. "Okay, let's go."

She stepped on the gas and cranked it up to twenty-two miles per hour. Thankfully, not too many other cars were out at 11:45 on a Monday night in the middle of an ice storm, go figure.

We didn't even get to Fran's.

It was hard to see at first. The freezing rain had just turned into plain rain, but it was hard and driving. The windshield wipers were going full speed.

Then we saw him.

There, up ahead, right in the middle of the intersection, in the centre of the four corners of St. Clair Avenue and Yonge Street, stood my father.

Drunk as a skunk.

Directing traffic.

"Pull over, Madison."

Apparently, she hadn't had any "pull over" lessons yet, so we agreed that idling the car somewhat nearish to the curb would be fine. Neither of us knew where the hazard lights were, so I flicked on the left-turn indicator. Then we just sort of sat there for a bit, watching Papa swaying in the intersection. He would hold up his arm very dramatically to stop the traffic on the red light and then swing it with wild enthusiasm on the green to get them going. The crazy thing was that, even though he was always a few beats behind the light, the cars waited for his signal before they proceeded.

Neither of us said anything as we watched.

Finally, I opened my door and Madison opened hers.

"I better do this myself," I said with as much authority as I could call up.

"My ass you will."

We both got out in the pounding rain.

"Papa?" I called.

"Mr. Kandinsky?" she called.

There was no hearing us in the rain and the rolling swish and whoosh of the cars driving by.

We were drenched after a few steps. I grabbed Madison's arm. "He really is a very sweet drunk," I screamed.

She nodded uncertainly but was game to go anyway.

"No, everybody says, really."

She nodded again. "Mr. Kandinsky?"

"Papa?"

He was in his suit jacket, no overcoat. God only knows where he had left it.

"Papa?"

He turned and saw me. Saw us. Big, big smile.

"Princessa!" He turned toward us. Unsteadily. "And the beautiful Madison!" Papa bowed elaborately. Traffic stopped on all four corners. The cars were confused. They waited patiently for their instructions.

"The lights work again, Mr. Kandinsky." Madison took one arm. I took the other. "They sent us to tell you that, that, they're very grateful for your help and you can go home now, sir. We'd be pleased to take you."

Papa nodded, well pleased with himself. "It's just like the old country."

"Yes, sir," she shouted. "That's what they said."

I didn't say anything. I was crying again.

Where *does* it all come from?

Papa got into the back seat as sweet as could be and started singing Polish songs to himself. I left Madison and Papa together and ran into Fran's to use the pay phone. The waitress took one look at me and insisted I use the restaurant phone. After three tries, I finally got through and told Auntie Eva, in point form, what had happened, that we were coming home now, and to call off the posse.

This was greeted by a fairly intense diatribe, mostly in Hungarian, ending with, "You make sure you are going very slowly on za streets. If you die because of him, I vill hunt you down and kill you myself."

"He really does have a very nice voice, you know," said Madison, as soon as I got back into the car. Papa had moved on to Broadway show tunes. We were treated to the second act of *Camelot*.

I was cross-eyed with the cold. Even though the Mercedes's fan was still cranked up as high as it could go, we had yet to rediscover the heat button. Madison and I shivered all the way home, but at least I could barely hear Papa.

It was 12:35 A.M. when we got back.

Luigi and Mike were in the lobby waiting for us. They grabbed up Papa mid-ballad. He was still cycling through the *Camelot* score as we got on the elevator.

"Tanks be to God, you are alive!" bellowed Auntie Eva, yanking open the door. Madison and I were bear hugged at the same time. Then she turned to Papa. "You too." Everyone else was in the living room having coffee and sandwiches. It was like a party, but not.

"And good evening to you, fair Eva!" Papa executed an elaborate, if sloppy, bow. I held my breath. It was even odds that Auntie Eva would clock him one. "You look as formidably formidable as always. Isn't *Camelot* a splendid movie, more than splendid, it's that splendid, isn't it? It's our Magda's favourite. When Richard Harris . . ."

Smoke was coming out of Auntie Eva's ears. She started toward him.

Mama got there first. She turned to Madison and mouthed "thank you." She gently took one of Papa's arms. Auntie Radmila strode over and, not so gently, took the other. They headed for the bedroom. Auntie Eva huffed off and planted herself firmly in the kitchen. It was like she was trying to hold down the linoleum.

Sarah and Kit came to get us and offered up towels and a plate of cookies. They learn well, my Blondes. There's nothing like cookies to cap off a crisis. Mike handed us a coffee and then he and Luigi started sorting out the transportation issues.

Kit would drive Sarah home while Mike followed in Madison's Mercedes with Madison, who would, in turn, be followed by Luigi and Auntie Luba in the white limo. After all the Blondes were properly dropped off, Luigi would somehow take care of the adults, but I wasn't paying attention by that point. They lost me at Sarah's house. I think I remembered to thank them before they left.

Mama and Auntie Radmila undressed Papa and stuck him in a hot shower. Auntie Eva could not be trusted with that task. She was safest in the kitchen wrestling with the floor.

"Buboola."

I turned to her. "Za skinny von . . ."

"Kit?"

"Ya, zat von." She grabbed a knife and started cutting more meat. For whom? Everyone had left.

"She told us." Big exhale. "Your Mama . . . she knows too."
Slice, slice, slice.

"Sorry?"

"She told us about za beautiful boy, about, about za situation." *Slice, slice.* "Zat *he* . . . your Papa, I mean, not za boy . . . alzough somevon should take a knife and chop off his . . . never mind. Zat your Papa . . .," she made fierce stabbing motions with the knife toward the bathroom, "should do zis ting *now* to you, ven, ven . . .," she gulped in some air, "ven you need . . ." *Slice, slice, slice.* "You should take a car and run over my heart, it is hurt so bad for you." Then she looked down at all the meat she had sliced and shook her head. "I am too sorry, my little Sophia."

She looked so little. It somehow dawned on me that the towering inferno that was my Auntie Eva wasn't even five feet three inches in her heels. I had never noticed that before.

I walked into the kitchen and put my arm around her. She was staring helplessly at all the meat. "Me too, Auntie Eva, me too."

Auntie Radmila opened the bathroom door and hustled an entirely compliant Papa into the bedroom. Even with the door shut we could hear Papa exhorting Auntie Radmila to "Run, John, run and tell them that there once was a place called Camelot!"

Instead of going in with them, Mama came into the kitchen.

"I am making you a bubble bat," she said.

Auntie Eva poured out a shot of brandy and handed it to me. "So you don't catch za cold."

Mama opened her mouth and Auntie Eva raised what was left of the unsliced kielbasa. "She iz not him! Keep it clean in your head, Magda. Za child iz not za fazer."

Whoa.

I had never heard any of the Aunties speak to Mama with anything but tenderness and deference.

Miraculously, Mama nodded, and then, even more mirac-ulously, said, "I know, Eva, I know." She put her arm around me. "I'll have one, too."

Okay, so, how was I supposed to decipher this wad of mixed messages? My teetotalling Mama and I walking arm in arm to the bathroom, brandies in hand, after rescuing my father from his forty-eight-hour bender. She looked away as I climbed into the tub and drew all the lavender-scented bubbles around me. Then Mama pulled down the toilet seat and sat down.

And that was okay.

Really.

I wanted her there. Mama said she'd hand me the glass whenever I wanted, but I didn't want it. I was in a bathtub filled with bubbles and my Mama was there. Mama wouldn't let anything else bad happen.

I lay back and closed my eyes.

I could hear Mama take a swig and shudder. "Kit told us about your Luke."

"I know." I kept my eyes closed. It was warm, I was safe, and Mama was there.

"He is a good boy, Sophie."

I dunked my head under water and came up again.

"He has honour, Sophie. He is a man. At eighteen, he is more a man den . . . more den . . ."

"I'm such an idiot, Mama! Stupid, stupid . . ."

"No!" She was beside the tub in a shot. "No, Sophie. He made a bad mistake, but it is right vat he does. You loved vell. Remember dat! Do not mistrust your judgment, Sophie, *your* judgment is first class."

"But he's going to marry her!" I wailed. "He said he loved me and he was going to break up with her and, Mama . . . he is going to *marry* her!"

She leaned over the tub and grabbed me. Mama was covered in bubbles and she kept hugging me until I hugged back.

And finally, after all that, I cried, one, more, time. Mama held on until I was finished.

"He vas crazy for you, Sophie. I, too, saw at da vedding, ve all saw." She grabbed a towel and patted herself here and there. "But he is a man, a full man, and he does vat a man must do. Sophie . . .," her gaze bore into me, "you chose vell, you choose vell. Za Blondes, your Madison, za beautiful boy . . . zese are good people, first-class-type people, real people. I am so proud of you and I am going to make you proud of me."

I shivered in the water.

"Mama, I am, I mean . . . about Papa."

She put her finger to her lips and shook her head.

There was, in that small gesture, hours of unspoken words. Jesus, I felt a hundred.

I dunked myself down under the water again for a long, long time and came up.

And my Mama was still there.

Luke got married three days ago.

Apparently.

He's going to come back to school to finish high school and graduate, but the newly minted Mrs. Pearson is not. Coming back that is. Or graduating.

The new Mrs. Pearson is *très occupé* setting up their newly-wed basement apartment in the Dupont and Christie streets area. And getting ready for the baby, of course. Both sets of parents are "helping the kids out." Therefore, Mrs. Luke Pearson feels no pressing need to get her diploma since she now has a husband *and* soon-to-be new baby. There are linens and bedding to pick out, all in a peach and powder blue theme.

I found this all out at Madison's. We went for a sleepover on the Friday night. It was the first one we'd had at Madison's since school started. We turned down a seniors' party at Eddie

Morgan's. I wasn't up for it. Sarah worried for a second about the consequences of not at least making an appearance, but she was mollified by Kit's insistence that it'll just make them want us more.

I didn't go to school for the rest of the week. I said I had a cold, what with dragging Papa in out of the rain and all. And even though I didn't sneeze or even sniffle once, Mama didn't call me on it. We were all pretty busy having our individual meltdowns at the Kandinsky household. It was like the island of Mama, the island of Papa, and the island of me. There was a lot of water separating us.

I watched old movies on TV all day and night, that and *The Price Is Right*. That Bob Barker guy is brilliant in a totally soothing, hey, everything-is-safe-and-cozy-in-your-world-so-long-as-you-are-watching-me kind of way. I defy anyone not to get totally swept up and away into the heart-pounding drama of "Showcase Showdown." Really, they should give that guy the Pulitzer or something.

When Mama wasn't working, she went with Papa to doctors appointments. There was no shouting. Mama wasn't rabid, nor did she shut down or retreat to her bed. Papa didn't touch a drop. We were all very civil, the islands of us.

They were both out when I left for Madison's. I left a note.

I said where I was and I said that I loved them both very much.

Because I did.

But I was so sick of them.

I was going to turn sixteen in February. For my sixteenth birthday, I wanted to be sixteen—not thirty-seven.

I also wanted some serious sympathy and non-stop attention over *my stuff.* I needed the world, okay, *my parents,* to
revolve around me for a while and to hell with their stuff.

I know that wasn't very "nice" or "sensitive." I know,
because I actually wrote it in my diary today, and it hit me
immediately how self-absorbed it looked, especially in crayon.
What kind of person, daughter, human was I?

But then again, I was the kid.

They were the adults.

So, the whole time I was home, I didn't run interference
for either of them, apologize for either of them, or lie for
either of them. I did not get onto the Auntie hotline and get
the Aunties stuck into solving us.

Because . . .

Because it hit me even before Madison and I got out of the
car that night. While we were still sitting in jaw-dropping
stunned stupidity at the sight of my father, four sheets to the
wind, directing traffic in the winter rain.

This was *not* my crisis.

It was Papa's.

Oh, I know it affects me and I'm in it and everything. But
it's not *my* crisis. It's *their* goddamned crisis and *they* have to
fix it.

Or not.

I had my hands full just dealing with the nauseating fact
that the brand new *Mrs.* Pearson was going from department
store to department store picking out peach and blue bath
towels.

I hate peach.

The Blondes called me every evening at one-and-a-half-hour intervals. Madison had worked out a schedule that she felt was a decent combination of watchfulness and care but short of harassment. They all also gave me fresh new bits from the outside world, so it wasn't just a stupefying litany of "So, how are you. Are you okay?" Hence, I was completely caught up on the Pearson nuptials and that the school was running about five to one that Alison Hoover had shamelessly "trapped" poor Luke Pearson. I had nothing to worry about in terms of my part in the whole thing, because other than the Blondes, no one else in the whole school knew anything about my part.

I was a secret.

Apparently.

The sleepover was going to be Madison's big truth-telling session. That was her Thursday, 7:47 P.M. bit of news. She said she was ready, she had promised, and, besides, everybody else had coughed up stuff that was at least as bad, hell, worse even.

So, according to Madison, she was going to lay out the whole deal. She practised various versions of this on me and we both decided that it was best to keep it simple, with lots of long pauses between facts.

Well, this ought to take my mind off me for a minute. Actually, it could be right up there with "Showcase Showdown."

I was the first to arrive.

Madison yanked me in the door before I could knock. "Thank God it's you. Youlookgoodreallyreally," she said. "I think I need a Valium. My parents had Edna over again last night and, and, I know they're doing this because of me, but between the farting and the rye and Cokes and the Burger Inn stories and OHMYGOD, you just should have seen her, she's so . . . oh damn, Kit's here."

Kit walked in and threw her arms around me. "It's official. The whole school thinks that Alison is a conniving slut and that she nailed a boy who showed all the signs of dumping her for someone else." Madison raised an eyebrow. "I swear! I've kept my ear on the tom-toms all week."

She kissed my head. "She'll burn in hell, Sophie, but the kid will have a father." We all stood around drinking this in, until Sarah bounced into the doorway.

"Okay, group hug!"

"Go to hell, Sarah," said Kit.

"Come on, come on, come on!"

"Good idea," said Madison.

So we hugged.

Then we went straight upstairs to Madison's room, which I'd almost forgotten is bigger than our entire condo. Mr. and Mrs. Chandler and the Judge were all out at some gala. They *had* to go since they were sponsoring the table, she said.

We all nodded.

I didn't know what she was talking about.

Fabi had laid out all our favourites, ketchup chips for the Blondes, a bowl of salt and vinegar chips for me, cheese popcorn, Doritos, Hostess Twinkies, Jos. Louis, and a case of Coke in bottles, not cans. Madison had carefully prepared all of the paraphernalia for our manicure/pedicure session. There was a fierce comfort in this. No matter what went on in the world, or even in our world, we did what we always did when we were alone together. We ate, we plotted, and we did our nails.

Madison cracked open a window, and she and Kit snuck their first cigarette of evening. Sarah had quit when she thought she was pregnant and never got into it again. It was nice to have someone with me. With two, you can sit around and feel righteous. When it was only me, I just felt left out.

"How's it hanging at your place, Soph?" Kit asked in between puffs. She shivered. The rain of Tuesday night had frozen up again and it was dead cold outside.

"Still eerily calm," I shrugged. "And yesterday, just before they got ready to go someplace, Mama said that she loved me."

"Yeah, so?" said Kit.

Madison kicked her.

"Ow!"

"No, it's just . . .," I got up and retrieved one of the nail polish bottles. "I mean, hell, I know she loves me, too much even, it's just that she's never said it before. It was weird, you know?"

They all nodded. They didn't have a clue what I was talking about. Each and every one of them, including Kit with her mom in California, had grown up on a steady diet of "I love you, darling." But then again, they were just as nuts as I was.

Hell, more.

Madison popped herself off of the ledge. "I, uh . . . Kit, shut the window please. I want to, uh . . ."

Kit shut the window and followed Madison back to Sarah and me on the rug. "What's up, fearless leader?"

Madison looked at me and then looked away.

I knew then.

"Well, Sophie knows this and, well, it's, uh, time that, given, what the hell, given all the, uh . . ."

Side glance at me.

"The thing is, what you guys didn't, well, not Sophie, she knows, well, what you couldn't possibly have known, is that the thing is . . . well, I am adopted."

Absolutely no response. Nothing.

"See, my parents . . ." She picked up the nail polish remover and then put it down again. "They, uh, adopted me when I was a baby, and, well, there you have it. I am not a Chandler by birth."

"Holy shit!" said Kit, who could always be counted on for the perfect response.

"I can't believe it!" Sarah got up and threw her arms around Madison. "It must have been so hard for you to know that and, my God. Do you know anything about your parents, I mean your real mom, not that your mom is not your real mom for heaven's sake, and what do they call the real mom by the way, there's, like, a word . . .?"

"Biological," said Kit as she got up and pulled out another cigarette, heading for the window again. "Put some periods in your sentences, Sarah. Well, they must have got you from the 'aristocratic accidents' section of the adoption catalogue."

"Kit!" said Sarah.

"Yeah, yeah," she shrugged and walked over to me. "I knew you were holding for her, Soph."

She lit the cigarette right in front of me, while I was looking up at her. "It's okay." She exhaled and headed for the window. "Hell, rosebud, you were holding for all of us. I don't know how your head didn't explode."

I nodded ironically. I think. I may have to practise that one in the mirror some more.

Kit knew there was more. She could smell it. She sat on the window ledge, addressed Madison, but looked at me. "So, do you know the deal on your biologicals?"

Madison stood up and went to the window with Kit, sharing her cigarette. "I'm not ready to explore all of that yet." She hugged herself.

Nicely done.

Not a lie, exactly.

She really was very good.

Sarah went on to cite whole paragraphs straight out of the Planned Parenthood brochure about how adoption is secret and the files are closed unless there is a compelling genetic issue and then there's "this whole long complicated process."

Kit said that her so-called "real" mother couldn't cut it either, when you come to think of it. "I mean she takes off to California just as I'm just starting high school. What kind of 'real mother' is that?"

We all agreed that it seemed to us that Kit's dad was doing a fine job of being a real mother. He let her have sleepovers whenever she wanted, went to all the teacher things, bought her Tampax in emergencies, and made her go to her shrink appointments most of the time.

We also all agreed that my mother had her hands full at the moment.

And we left it at that.

Sarah had the most regular-type mom of the group, so she was silent on that front, but since she had almost become a mother, at least in her head, she had the most to say and she did, all night long. We also spent hours fantasizing about how we were going to raise our daughters. We, the enlightened and sensitive generation, would raise *our* daughters in the spirit of open honesty and no pressure. We would be loving but not smothering. We'd be supportive but never embarrassing. Above all, we'd remember what it was like to be a teen with the weight of a complex, confusing world on our shoulders and we would do all this while maintaining our good looks and not "let ourselves go."

And it didn't bother me that Madison copped out.

Really.

What a group. I looked from Blonde to Blonde. Each one of us was at best, at least a little damaged, changed by our secrets. Individually, we were kind of wobbly—together, we were a miracle. I had experienced it first hand. When we were together, there was a force field around us.

I was, finally, "completely clean" with them. The Blondes now knew about every stinking messed up part of my life and they had stuck in, hard. Madison wouldn't feel the power I felt from that.

She just couldn't get up to do it. She just couldn't lay out the story of her addict mom and poor old Edna.

And I understood that.

Maybe I even loved her more for it.

But the universe shifted in the not telling.

I, Sophie Kandinsky, was now the strong one.

At around midnight, we broke into the back of the Chandler bar and retrieved a Southern Comfort bottle, which Madison swore wouldn't be missed since she'd never seen her parents, or their friends, touch the stuff. I stuck to soft drinks.

It hit me on my third ginger ale that we were sort of like the next generation of Mama and the Aunties and I said so.

They *loved* that.

"Hell, that's as good a goal as any to aspire to," said Kit.

And I loved that.

We sort of fell asleep where we landed, pillows and pop bottles everywhere. None of us were actually on the bed. We were scattered everywhere. Sarah, Madison, Kit, and I all fell asleep on the floor, just pillows, no blankets. They weren't necessary. We were covered by our force field.

24

I didn't get home until well after lunch.

No one was in the kitchen or living room.

"Mama? Papa?! I'm home. Anybody here?"

Papa walked out of the bedroom.

"Hi, Papa, we had a great time. Everyone, uh, says hi."

He was wearing his blue suit and his new white shirt. No tie though. His eyes were crystal clear, his hands steady.

Papa smiled. His hair fell into his eyes.

"Hello, Princess."

"Is Mama showing a house?"

I looked around the condo again. Everything was tidy. Dishes put away. The bed was made in their room. Laundry put away. No newspapers or books strewn around. Were we expecting company? And that's when I saw it. To the left of the front door.

A small tobacco-coloured suitcase.

"Papa?"

I swear my heart was thumping against my chest and in my ears to different beats.

I couldn't hear myself think.

"Papa, where's Mama? Papa, what's happening?"

He stepped toward me and smiled again. "Princess, it's okay, I told her that I wanted to do this alone."

"Do what? Papa, are you okay?"

He shook his head. "No, Princess, not really." He looked to the ceiling as if the words were going to be written up there. I looked up too. There was nothing but our cheap overhead condo globe. "I have been a very selfish man, Sophia, not just now, not just since I got out, since, since . . . for a long time."

Sophia. He always called me Sophia, no matter how many times I told him that it was really important that I be called Sophie. Sophie *was* me. Mama, who didn't even approve of the name change, got it straight right from the beginning. Even the Aunties scored at least fifty-fifty on remembering.

"Selfish? No, Papa, that's not fair, look at everything that's happened to you, my God!"

He raised his hand.

"I've been selfish and I have damaged the only people I love and care about in this whole world."

My head spun. It sounded like movie dialogue or something straight out of *Sweet Savage Love*. Real people don't actually talk like that to other real people. Had he been practising in front of the mirror all morning?

"I am so sorry, Sophia. I had no right."

"Sophie," I said.

"What?"

"It's Sophie now, you always forget."

He ignored that. "You see, the situation is that your Mama and me, we've been to see doctors and counsellors all this week. We, I have been going to these meetings. Your Mama has been going to something called Al-Anon since before the wedding."

It was too much. I zoned out for a second and just listened to all that pumping and chugging that was going on inside of me.

"And the worst thing is that I've unconsciously made you a partner in, in, my, uh, my relationship with alcohol." He crumbled a bit. "Apparently, I did this before as well. I won't ask for your forgiveness now, or Mama's, but one day. One day soon," he smiled. "This is my goal in sobriety."

I remembered last night and Sarah citing chapter and verse to us from the Planned Parenthood literature that she had picked up to "remind" herself. Had Papa swallowed an Alcoholics Anonymous pamphlet?

"Yeah, okay." I nodded. "But what's going on? What is the suitcase doing . . . Papa, you've been under so much stress and Mama has been pushing you . . ."

"Princess, I'm a drunk and . . .," he shut his eyes, "and that's the truth."

"But you're sober now. You've been sober all week, I can tell, I can always tell. It's been days now. And then there were all those years, years, Papa, in prison, where you didn't drink at all. You'll be fine now. We'll tell Mama."

He shook his head. "Sophia, please, please, let me say this while I still have the courage. The truth . . . is that I *am* an alcoholic. I've been sober for days before, for weeks. I have sworn to your Mama, a hundred times, when you were a baby, when you were little, oh, Sophia, before you were even born. I've even been sober for months at a time."

"For years!" I corrected. "In prison."

"No, Sophia." He touched my cheek. "Those years in Kingston, in the prison, see, there are ways . . ."

I fell rather than sat down onto the couch. Papa crouched down in front of me.

"No more lies, Princess." He placed his hands on my knees. "It's time for me to do this. Mama didn't ask me to leave. This is my decision and I won't come back until I am well, until I know I will no longer hurt the two of you." He looked back up to the ceiling. "And if you'll both have me."

"You? *You* want to leave?"

"I'll be going to these meetings. Every day until, well, until I don't have to go every day and then I will go every couple of days until I can go a little less. But, Sophia, I will have to go for the rest of my life. I know that now and I needed to know that. I have to leave to get well. I need to live with the truth of what I am."

I opened my mouth to protest. He could do it from home, we would help, it would be easier. We could all make it work for him.

But the words refused to come out. They evaporated on my tongue.

"I couldn't love you or Mama more and for once in my life, I need to be a man about this and fix it for all of us. It won't be for forever, Sophia."

Sophie, damn it. Why was that bothering me so much? I'd barely noticed it all this time.

"Where are you going to go?"

He shook his head and then smiled again. "Well, you won't believe this, but Auntie Eva is letting me live in her basement apartment, rent free. For however long it takes, she said, 'until you are drying yourself out or you find God or vatever you sober drunks do.'"

It was like she was in the room with us. Okay, okay, Auntie Eva's. It wasn't the other side of the moon, it was on Davenport Road. I could go and visit whenever I wanted, and this time I would. I was still having trouble breathing.

"Auntie Eva, eh? Your mortal enemy?"

Papa shrugged. "The brandy made her an enemy. That woman is a force of nature, all of those crazy ladies and your friends too, Sophia. You have the best . . . you deserve the best."

He got up. "Walk me to the elevator." Papa held out his hand. I took it and he yanked me up effortlessly.

He picked up his suitcase and we went into the corridor. He walked just a little ahead of me until he got to the elevators, and then Papa turned.

Time stopped.

Papa was silhouetted in the long narrow hallway, backlit by the small north window at the end.

All those broken . . . everything.

And he was still beautiful.

He pressed for the elevator and it appeared immediately. Papa stood in the entrance so the doors wouldn't shut. He shook his head. "Don't come down. I couldn't bear it, Sophia."

I was just about to forget about everything and run into him, colliding deep and hard into the beautiful suit of his and holding on for dear life. Like all those months ago at the prison. But I was so, so much younger then. The elevator buzzer started going off.

Brrring, brrring, brrring.

"It's Sophie, Papa, not Sophia. There is no Sophia any more."

"Yes, of course, yes." He reached over and kissed my forehead over and over again. "I will get better, Sophie. I will do better. I promise."

I stopped breathing.

Papa stepped back but still held on to me.

"I mean it this time. Do you believe me? I need you to believe me . . . *Sophie.*"

Brrring, brrring, brrring.

He stepped back into the elevator.

"Yes, Papa. I believe . . ."

He blew me a kiss just as the elevator shut.

"I believe that you believe it," I said to the doors.

And then . . . I started to breathe again.

Acknowledgments

I believe that writing is a solitary and lonely pursuit. Given that conviction, imagine my surprise when I turned my thoughts to the acknowledgments, only to discover that it is a rather long list. Ken, Nikki, and Sasha Toten were insightful first readers. Margaret Morin gave me pieces of her life to play with. My "Goup," Nancy Hartry, Susan Adach, Loris Lesynski, and Ann Goldring, consistently inspired me. Paula Wing was present at the creation. Scott Fenton offered criminally good advice, and Leona Trainer offered steadfast encouragement. Then there is the intelligence and talent at Penguin, including Tracy Bordian, Dawn Hunter, Lisa LaPointe, Karen McMullin-Hall, and Barbara Berson, who made it all happen.

Mike and Nicky Meanchoff are the original and wonderful proprietors of the "real" Homeway Soda Bar on Mount Pleasant Road. Although Sophie's Mike is entirely fictional, I hope that the best of Mike Meanchoff's larger-than-life essence was somehow captured in Sophie's Mike. I also want to thank Jeannie Carter, Kathy Davis, and Lesley Boyle, my high school "Blondes." And speaking of high school, there could not have been a better one than Northern Secondary.

Finally, I joyously acknowledge "the queen of historical romance," Rosemary Rogers, and her delicious 1974 novel *Sweet Savage Love,* which played such a large part in both Sophie's and my own coming of age. I was then, as I am now, a fan.